BAD BLOOD

☆

Shank Hollis didn't want killing, but Torn could almost smell it coming, and odds were that Drew Mitchell was going to wind up becoming one of the casualties.

"Baylis, you keep a close eye on Torn," said Hollis.

"You can count on me, Shank."

Baylis stepped sideways to lock the door. "Hope you don't try nothing. I'd rather not have a price on my head."

Turning slightly so that Baylis could not detect the movement of his arm, Torn slowly slipped his right hand under his frock coat. A flick of the thumb removed the strap holding his saber-knife upside-down in its sheath. The weapon fell into his hand.

"You've got me dead to rights," said Torn. "What can I do?"

"Not a damn thing," agreed Baylis, sounding relieved. Convinced that Torn was going to be sensible, he relaxed a notch or two.

Torn whirled and threw the saber-knife.

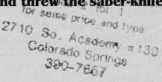

Also by Hank Edwards

THE JUDGE

WAR CLOUDS

GUN GLORY

TEXAS FEUD

STEEL JUSTICE

LAWLESS LAND

Published by
HARPERPAPERBACKS

HANK EDWARDS

THE JUDGE

BAD BLOOD

HarperPaperbacks
A Division of HarperCollins*Publishers*

This is a work of fiction. The characters, incidents, and dialogues are products of the author's imagination and are not to be construed as real. Any resemblance to actual events or persons, living or dead, is entirely coincidental.

HarperPaperbacks *A Division of* HarperCollins*Publishers*
10 East 53rd Street, New York, N.Y. 10022

Cover illustration by Bill Maughan

First printing: May 1992

Printed in the United States of America

HarperPaperbacks and colophon are trademarks of HarperCollins*Publishers*

10 9 8 7 6 5 4 3 2 1

CHAPTER

1

WHEN SHERIFF DREW MITCHELL CROSSED THE DEAD-LINE OF Ellsworth, Kansas, the "Texas" side of the trail town was going great guns. He figured at least a hundred horses stood at hitching posts all along both sides of Kiowa Street. And for every horse there was one half-wild, crazy-proud Texas cowboy to contend with.

Mitchell squared broad shoulders, stepped out into the middle of the street, and started south with long, easy strides. He carried a Remington ten-gauge sawed-off cradled in his left arm. His right hand swung free, never far from the .44 Dance holstered on his hip.

Lamplight poured through the windows and doors of Ellsworth's twelve saloons and four dance halls, falling in long mustard-yellow splotches on the rutted hardpan of the street. The endless thunder of bootheels on floor planks, punctuated by lusty whoops and hollers, came from the dance halls, where the cowboys capered with world-weary percentage girls to the rhythms of reel and gallopade. More cowboys were packed like sardines into the saloons, belly-up to the bars and hash counters or sitting at deal tables and losing their hard-earned wages to cardsharps. Even more filled the boardwalks, going from place to place, laughing or cursing, steady or staggering, but always with that rolling horse-warped swagger and with spurs a-jingling—that sound a cowboy most loved to hear.

Mitchell prowled, alert for trouble. He didn't want any, but it was his job to find it and deal with it when it happened. He was a tall, rangy man with steady nerves, hard fists, and a good head on his shoulders. He was confident in his ability to handle any situation, and had a right to be.

The first stars were appearing in the purple sky of early evening. Behind him, north of the dead-line, the respectable side of Ellsworth was quiet, orderly, peaceful. Folks were sitting down to dinner now, looking forward to a pleasant evening at home with family and friends.

Mitchell had just finished his own supper—had just kissed his young, pretty wife good night. It was going to be a long night on the Texas side. Things wouldn't taper off down here until well after midnight. And when he finally got home, Jenny would be asleep.

For a moment Mitchell's attention strayed from the business at hand. He was a lucky man—the luckiest man in Kansas—to have a wife like Jenny. His friend Clay Torn had said so himself. Not that he needed telling. Clay had stood as Drew's best man at the church wedding three months ago. Three months—and Mitchell still couldn't believe he'd been so lucky.

Jenny was a wonderful girl, sensible and brave, but

she worried about him, about his dangerous job. He saw the worry in her eyes every night when he strapped on his side gun, picked up the sawed-off, and kissed her good night. Although she never spoke of her fears, he knew she was wondering if it was a kiss good night or a good-bye forever, and that bothered him.

But Mitchell didn't know what to do about it. He'd been a badge toter most of his adult life. He took pride in his work. He knew he wasn't cut out for farming or cowpunching. He thrived on the risk and challenge.

A lawman in a trail town like Ellsworth ran big risks every day he kept that piece of five-pointed tin pinned to his shirt. Every year dozens of cattle herds, thousands of Texas longhorns bound for eastern slaughterhouses or new northern ranges, came to Ellsworth up the Chisholm Trail. And with the herds came hundreds of Texas cowboys, tough and untamed. After three months on the trail, they were ready to cut loose. The Texas side of Ellsworth caught hell every year. Mitchell's job was to keep the lid on.

A lot of the men who tried trail-town troubleshooting died young. This was Mitchell's third season as Ellsworth's tin star, and the fact that he'd held the position so long said a lot about the man. He had the reputation, and the cowboys knew he wasn't a man to cross.

They watched him now as he strolled down Kiowa, through the splotches of lamplight. Mitchell felt their hard, bright stares. There was a certain amount of hostility and resentment in those stares, but he didn't take it personally. The cowboys disliked what the man represented, not the man himself. They were full of pride and vinegar, and no Texas cowboy worth his salt liked to admit that any man held sway over him. Mitchell understood this, and he tried not to push them too hard. As long as they played by the rules, he let them play.

As he passed the Alamo Saloon three drovers stormed through the batwings, staggering like new-born foals. The batwings cracked back on their hinges, a sharp and sudden sound not unlike gunfire. Mitchell tensed in reflex, half crouching, and swung that way. The three cowboys spotted him, and the badge and the shotgun sobered them some. Striking nonchalant poses on the boardwalk, they stood and watched him, wary and still as deer. Mitchell relaxed, nodded slightly, and moved on.

They crossed the street behind him—the jingle-jangle of their spurs told him this. He took a half-dozen steps before glancing back. As they moved through a patch of lamplight he saw for the first time that they were packing iron strapped to their chap-covered legs. Turning, he angled across the street to cut them off. They saw him coming and pulled up on the boardwalk in front of the Red Dog, another watering hole directly across the street from the Alamo. Mitchell stopped ten feet away from them, giving them space. Not that he was afraid. A man who let fear rule him could not survive as a trail-town lawman. But like the ornery long-horns from which they made their livings, Texas cowboys hated to be crowded, and Mitchell respected that.

"You boys heading back to your night camp?"

One of the cowboys made a production of perusing the front of the Red Dog.

"Looks like a saloon to me, not no night camp."

One of the others chuckled. "I declare, Clete, you're a card."

The third cowboy just stood and stared at Mitchell, unblinking and inscrutable, his eyes whiskey dull. He swayed like a sapling in a stiff breeze.

"We've got a few rules here," said Mitchell amiably. "They're posted all over town, and my deputy rides out to every herd when it comes in and goes over those rules with the trail crews, just so's everyone understands. The first rule is this: You check your irons right away when you roll into town, and you don't pick 'em up until you're ready to pull your freight."

"You aimin' to try and take my gun, Sheriff?" Clete sneered. His voice was slurred, his tone belligerent.

Mitchell gave him a hard look. Clete was standing in the play of smoky light leaking through the Red Dog's doorway. He was a lanky, loose-limbed man who seemed to slouch even when standing. His features were narrow and surly. Strands of sweat-damp yellow hair clung to his brow. He was trying to grow some whiskers on his gaunt, sunburned cheeks, but it looked more like wispy yellow mold than honest face hair. A braided quirt dangled from his left wrist.

"That's whiskey talking," replied Mitchell sternly. "None of us wants trouble, do we?"

Clete's grin was about as pleasant as a wolf's snarl.

"Speak for yourself, mister," he said.

CHAPTER 2

MITCHELL KNEW THAT WHEN A COWBOY CALLED SOMEONE "mister" it was not a term of respect—just the opposite, in fact. But he didn't take offense. Clete was trying to rile him, and he wasn't going to play Clete's game.

"I ain't afraid of you," added Clete, impudent. "I ain't afraid of nothing and nobody."

"You don't have anything to be afraid of," replied Mitchell. "So why do you lug all that gun weight around?"

"Don't try putting a tight rein on me, lawman."

Mitchell's lips thinned in a cold smile. The cowboy who had been chuckling a moment before suddenly looked stone-cold sober. He saw something in the sheriff that Clete was too drunk or too vainglorious to see.

"Come on, Clete," he murmured, deferential. "Shank said no trouble."

"Shank can eat corral dust," railed the quarrelsome Clete. "He ain't my boss."

Another cowboy exited the Red Dog and paused to study the confrontation, rolling a smoke. He was just a casual spectator, but he stood at Mitchell's flank, and that annoyed Mitchell.

"You ride with these boys?" snapped the lawman.

The cowboy shook his head, dropped the makings, and discreetly turned back inside the saloon.

"What outfit are you with?" Mitchell asked the three gunpackers.

"The Slash B," was Clete's defiant answer. "I'm—"

"You're crossing in deep water," said Mitchell. "Get back to your night camp. Come back tomorrow night only if you're willing to abide by the rules."

"Rules," jeered Clete. "Let me tell you what to do with—"

Mitchell racked the shotgun on his shoulder. The meaning of this action was not lost on the three Slash B riders.

Clete angrily slapped the quirt against his leg. "Let's go," he growled at his partners.

They started back across the street, to horses tied to one of the rails in front of the Alamo. Mitchell did not linger to watch them. He turned south again, as though he fully expected them to comply with his order. The trail-crew night camps were generally south of town, out on the prairie, where the herds were held until moved to the stockyards. Mitchell figured if they rode past him, that would be the end of it. Putting his back to them was a demonstration of cool nerve, with a dash of disdain added. Mitchell knew the Texas cowboy. In fact, he respected them. They were a rough and rowdy crowd, but he'd never met one with the makings of a backshooter.

But the man named Clete did not ride south. He savagely reined his cowpony in the opposite direction, raking with his spurs, slashing with the quirt, and letting loose a piercing yell as the horse lunged up Kiowa in the direction of the dead-line.

Mitchell whirled. The other two Slash-B riders sat their dancing mounts, dumbfounded. Three long, angry strides took Mitchell to the blood bay carrying the man who, only a few minutes ago, had been giggling drunkenly at Clete's smart remark. The cowboy didn't look as though he felt like laughing now. Mitchell reached up, grabbed a handful of shirt, and hauled the Texan to the ground.

"I need the loan of your horse," rasped the sheriff, vaulting into the saddle.

"Sure," mumbled the sprawled cowboy. He threw up an arm to shield his face from clods of dirt kicked up by the blood bay as Mitchell gadded the horse after Clete.

A gunshot ripped the night, and Mitchell bent low in the saddle. Then he realized Clete wasn't shooting at him. The cowboy fired twice more into the sky, whooping like a moonstruck coyote. A chorus of shouts accompanied the stampede of men out of establishments all along Kiowa Street.

When Clete crossed the dead-line, Mitchell felt a chill snake down his spine. Every cowboy knew a trail-town dead-line was just that—a line he did not cross unless he was willing to forfeit his life. It was a harsh rule, but one the respectable citizens expected their lawman to enforce. Almost all of Ellsworth's residents made their living off the Texas drover in one way or another, but precious few wanted to have anything to do with him personally.

Clete took the turn onto Main Street at a headlong gallop and was momentarily out of Mitchell's sight. The sheriff heard three more gunshots in quick succession before taking the corner himself. What he saw made him check the blood bay so sharply that the horse locked its front legs and almost sat down in the street.

Sam Tucker, the storekeeper, was sprawled half off the boardwalk in front of his shebang. Mitchell made note of the ax handle on the ground beside the body. Stunned and feeling a little sick, the sheriff tore his gaze away from Tucker's frighteningly still form and looked at Clete. The cowboy was no longer riding hell-for-leather. He was circling his pony, staring at Tucker and then the charcoal burner in his hand and then back at Tucker. He looked stunned, too.

"Drop it!" yelled Mitchell.

The sheriff's shout shook some sense into Clete. But panic moved in and took over as he realized what he'd done. As Mitchell kicked the blood bay forward the cowboy raised his pistol and pulled the trigger. The six-shooter dry-fired. Before Clete could get his mount straightened out, Mitchell was on him. The horses collided. Mitchell lunged and carried Clete out of his rig. The cowboy took the brunt of the fall. He put up a feeble resistance until Mitchell's fist slammed into his face.

Scooping up the scattergun he'd dropped in the fall, Mitchell glanced upstreet. Men were gathering around Sam Tucker. More were coming on the run from every direction. Tucker's wife stood rigidly on the boardwalk, screaming into the apron she'd pulled up to her face.

She and her husband lived on the second floor of the clapboard building that housed the Tucker store, and Mitchell realized that Sam must have come boiling out into the street to see what the shooting was about.

"My God!" someone yelled, strangle-voiced. "He's dead! Sam Tucker's dead!"

Moaning, Clete was trying to get up. Mitchell spun and stuck the shotgun in his face. The cowboy looked up into both barrels and became quite still.

"Mister, you're under arrest for murder," rasped Mitchell. "And God have mercy on you, because Judge Torn won't."

CHAPTER

3

When Federal Judge Clay Torn stepped off the west-bound train, it was still dark. The eastern rim of the sky was brightening, and pinwheeling strips of mare's-tail clouds were colored a vivid pink by the light of a sun that yet lingered below the horizon, but night shadows still enveloped the Ellsworth depot—shadows deepened by the cloud of black, sooty smoke billowing out of the Jupiter locomotive's diamond stack.

Torn touched the brim of his hat to a couple of sleepy-eyed calico queens disembarking from the day coach and sidestepped a portly peddler struggling with a pair of bulky valises.

"Judge Torn."

He turned and immediately recognized Curly Loomis, Ellsworth's deputy sheriff. As they shook hands Torn noticed that the usually good-natured Curly looked positively grim.

"What's wrong, Curly? Is Drew all right? Jenny?"

11

"They're fine, Judge, don't fret. There's been a killing. Happened just last night. A man named Sam Tucker. Ran a general store."

"Sam Tucker." Torn shook his head. "Don't think I knew him."

"Fine old gentleman. Always had a kind word for you. Never begrudged credit to anyone short on hard money. Everybody in town liked him."

"Then who killed him?"

Curly rubbed his bewhiskered jowls, but couldn't rub off the grimace.

"One of them wild and woolly Texas boys. The town's pretty riled."

"Which means an impartial jury will be as hard to come by as ice water in hell," mused Torn.

"Assuming the cowboy who done Sam in comes to trial."

"What do you mean by that, Curly?"

The deputy shrugged. "You know how it is. There's always lynch talk after something like this. But when they find out you're here, I reckon they'll settle down."

Torn's steel-cast gray eyes narrowed. Grim resolve sharpened the sun-bronzed lines of his clean-shaven face. He was a tall, lean man, dressed in a black frock coat, black trousers, and spurless boots, a black string tie closing the collar of a white shirt. Beneath his hat, wheat-colored hair was close-cropped.

He carried a small black leather valise, and strapped to the valise was a scabbard holding a Winchester 44/40 repeating rifle. On his hip was a Colt .45 Peacemaker. But the weapon Curly had come to associate with Clay Torn was concealed beneath the frock coat. Secured in a shoulder-harness rig under Torn's left arm was a knife. An extraordinary knife, as legendary in its own right as the man who carried it.

Curly knew the legend as well as anyone.

Scion of one of South Carolina's most influential families, Clayton Randall Torn had fought on the losing side in the War Between the States. Captured at Gettysburg, he had spent sixteen months in the living hell of a Union prisoner-of-war camp. The knife he now carried had once been a saber, the property of a sadistic Union sergeant assigned to that camp. Torn had killed the sergeant while making his escape. Later, the saber had been broken, and Torn had honed what remained down to fifteen inches of razor-sharp steel.

Hunted by federal patrols with orders to kill on sight, Torn had made his way through the shambles of a dying Confederacy, returning to South Carolina to find his family dead and Ravenoak, the ancestral Torn home, burned to the ground by Sherman's pillaging bluecoats. Worse still, Torn had learned that his fiancée, Melony Hancock, had been abducted by Yankee deserters.

Torn had followed Melony's kidnappers west, all the way to the lawless Indian nations. In his search for her, he'd cut a bloody swath through the host of outlaws populating the unassigned lands. He didn't find Melony, but he did redeem himself in the eyes of the federal government.

With the issue of secession settled, the nation had turned its attention to the frontier, where the two greatest obstacles to expansion were Indians and outlawry. While the army dealt with Indians, men like Torn were desperately needed to bring law and order to the West. Due to his prewar law studies at the prestigious University of Virginia, Torn was appointed to a federal judgeship. He was one of a handful of judges whose formidable task it was to dispense justice in a circuit that included Missouri, Arkansas, Kansas, Nebraska, and the Dakotas.

In Curly's opinion, Torn was different from most judges. His propensity for rendering judgment from the barrel of a gun, or the point of his saber knife, had earned him the fear and respect of badmen from Abilene to the Absarokas—as well as a certain amount of notoriety in more respectable circles.

But Curly Loomis didn't give two hoots whether respectable folks thought Clay Torn was little better than the desperadoes he dealt with. Torn was a natural-born fighter, and Ellsworth's deputy sheriff had a gut hunch one hell of a fight was just around the corner.

Curly had a nose for trouble, developed during his younger, leaner years as a freighter on the Santa Fe Trail. He'd sniffed out his share of redskin and bandit danger. In his opinion, not all the Indians and longriders west of the Mississippi could equal the kind of trouble a Texas cowboy could bring.

"Yes, sir," said Curly, "cowboys and Kansas just can't seem to mix, like oil and water. The good folks of Ellsworth have had it up to their eyebrows with wild Texicans, Judge. I reckon it won't be long before they throw 'em out, like they done back in Abilene."

"Abilene would still be just a patch of prairie had it not been for the cattle trade," said Torn. "Same goes for Ellsworth."

Curly nodded. "The folks don't mind taking the cowboy's money. They just don't want anything more to do with him after that, though. I think they'd like to make an example of this feller Drew's got locked up."

"There's nothing worse than men who are so convinced they're right that they'll do wrong to prove it," said Torn.

Curly scratched his head, puzzling over this comment.

"Got a buckboard yonder," said the deputy. "Take you into town if you like. Thing is, Drew asked me to stop by his house and look in on Jenny. He ain't been home all night."

Torn nodded. "I'd like to see her again. Say hello."

Curly noticed that Torn's smile was a little sad.

As they left the depot platform Torn spared two cowboys a passing glance. The Texans were tilted against the depot's shiplap wall. One was building a smoke. The other was sliding his boot across the weathered planks of the platform to hear his spur sing. He was also carving on the depot wall with a clasp knife. "/B" was the cowboy's graffiti.

Torn had no way of knowing it then, but he was going to have cause to remember that brand for the rest of his life.

The cowboys didn't seem to pay Torn the slightest notice. But once the buckboard pulled out onto the road leading into Ellsworth, an arrow's flight away, the cowboy with the roll-your-own now dangling from his lips shrugged away from the wall.

"Reckon one of us best go tell Shank," he drawled.

"You figure that's the judge, Baylis? The one that cattle buyer told Shank was due in?"

"I figure."

"Well, one of us has to stick near the telegraph office."

Baylis plucked the cigarette out of his teeth, dropped it, and ground it under a bootheel. He glanced over his shoulder at the telegraph-office window farther down the platform. He'd been with Shank Hollis, the Slash-B straw boss, when Shank had paid call on that window last night.

"It'll take a couple of days to get a wire back from Texas," he said. "Don't know why we got to ride herd on the telegraph every minute."

" 'Cause Shank says so. You go on. I'll stay here."

"Hell, we all know what Mr. Bartlett's going to want us to do. I say we go on and do it and dust out of this godforsaken place."

"We'll be making dust, okay." The other Slash B rider nodded. "After we bust Clete out of jail, we'll have all of Kansas stirred up like a hornet's nest."

CHAPTER 4

JENNY HUTCHINSON MITCHELL AWOKE TO DISCOVER THAT HER husband was not asleep beside her. He usually dragged home in the early-morning hours, dead tired, and slept late. It was her practice to rise early and have breakfast ready for him when he wakened.

Her first reaction to this change in routine was terror.

Maybe he was dead.

She lived with the fear of that happening every day. She'd married that fear, but she had to live with it, because she couldn't live without the man.

Now she jumped out of bed with a quiet sob—a pretty, slender woman with hair the color of mahogany and eyes the green of the sea. Throwing on a wrapper, she rushed into the front room of their little clapboard house on the outskirts of Ellsworth.

Someone was knocking on the door.

She threw it open to find Curly and Torn standing on the porch, silhouetted against the fiery sunrise.

The expression on her face startled both men. Torn was the first to put two and two together.

"It's not what you think, Jenny," he said. "Drew's fine."

A flood of relief left her weak, and she sagged against the doorframe, covering her face with both hands. Torn stepped forward and put an arm around her shoulders. Curly's first thought was that this was being mighty familiar with another man's wife. Then he remembered that Drew and Jenny and Torn went way back.

"Drew sent me down to tell you everything's all right, ma'am," said Curly. "He thought you might still be asleep, so he told me to swing by the depot first to see if the judge came in on the morning train."

Jenny smiled bravely at Torn and composed herself. "Please come in. I'll . . . I'll make some coffee."

They stepped into the two-room house. It was Torn's first visit to the Mitchell house. Drew had bought the place shortly after the marriage. Before that, the sheriff had been living in a hotel room and Jenny had been staying at a boardinghouse.

The room was small, but neat and comfortable, with the kitchen to the right, a table in the center, and a couple of upholstered wing chairs around the fireplace to the left. The furniture looked rough and secondhand, and the house itself was not the most sound—structures in a boomtown like Ellsworth tended to be thrown together in a slapdash way. But the place was clean, and had nice little touches: the hearth rug beneath the chairs, curtains on the windows, an arrangement of wildflowers in a green bottle on the table. And

Torn was reminded that though the house was small and somewhat run-down, it was also a home, and a home was something he didn't have.

"Begging your pardon, ma'am," said Curly, sitting at the table with Torn and solicitously watching Jenny as she made the coffee, "but you had a bad shock there. Want I should fetch the doc?"

"That won't be necessary. Thanks just the same, Curly."

"I just thought, with that little one you're carryin' and all . . ." Curly's bristly jowls turned a deep shade of crimson. He had little experience with women and felt acutely self-conscious around them. But that didn't keep him from thinking that Jenny Mitchell was the prettiest lady in Kansas and that Drew had done himself proud.

"What?" asked Torn. "What was that?"

Jenny turned and smiled sweetly. "Of course, you couldn't know. Drew and I are going to have a child. We never know where you are, Clay, so we couldn't send word."

"That's wonderful news, Jenny."

She put an enamel pot filled with water on the stove, stirred up the coals with an iron poker, and added two small pieces of wood. Grinding up the coffee, she put two handfuls in the pot and came to the table to sit with them.

"The coffee will take a while," she said. "Wood costs a lot of money out here, since it has to be freighted in. Everything costs too much." She saw the sympathy on Torn's face and changed the subject, turning to Curly. "What happened last night, Curly? Why couldn't Drew come home?"

Curly grimaced. "Some drunken Texas hooligan was shooting up the town and killed Sam Tucker in the process."

"Oh, no! Poor Eunice Tucker!"

"Drew's got the cowboy locked up in the jail. He thought he'd best keep an eye on him overnight. The townfolk were getting all worked up, and you know Drew won't stand for no vigilante justice."

"Sometimes I think we'd be better off if those herds went somewhere else," said Jenny.

Curly glanced at Torn. "Me and the judge were just talking about that. Folks don't want to live with the cowboys, but they don't know if they could live without 'em. Ellsworth might just dry up and blow away."

Jenny sighed. "Yes, and I suppose Drew would go to the next trail town that pops up out of the prairie, and it would start all over again." Resigned, she stood and turned to the bedroom door. "Help yourself to the coffee when it's ready. I'm going to get dressed." She laughed. "What would my husband think if he saw me like this with two gentlemen callers?" She stopped suddenly, came back to put a hand on Torn's shoulder. "I'm glad you're here, Clay," she said in a small voice. "I'd be glad even if there wasn't trouble. But since there is, I'm doubly glad."

"Don't worry," said Torn. It was all he could think to say, and he knew it wasn't enough. He cared about Jenny. More than he was willing to admit even to himself. And it bothered him that she wasn't as happy as she could be—as she deserved to be. She put on a brave front, but he could see right through it.

"I reckon you'll be heading into town to see Drew,"

said Curly. "I'd be obliged if you'd allow me to drive you in. I brought a buckboard over from the livery."

Jenny started to protest, but realized her husband was behind Curly's offer. Drew had known she would come to the jail to see with her own eyes that he was all right. Of course, she was perfectly able to take care of herself. But this was just like Drew. Though she was only a couple of months into the pregnancy, Drew was determined to pamper her. Hence Curly's bringing the buckboard. To refuse the offer would smack of ingratitude.

"I won't be long," she promised.

After the bedroom door closed behind her, the two men sat in silence a moment, sharing similar thoughts. It was Curly who spoke up first, shaking his head ruefully.

"Drew's a lucky man. He's also a darned fine lawman. One of the best I've ever known. It ain't none of my business, Judge, but it seems to me like a man who's got a wife like Jenny—and a child coming, in the bargain—shouldn't pin a tin star on his shirt and go out and risk his life every day. There ought to be a law against that kind of thing."

Torn smiled. "It would be a good law."

Curly leaned forward, lowering his voice so that it would not carry into the next room. "Maybe you could talk some sense into him."

Torn drew a long breath, let it out slow. "I ought to, Curly. I feel the same way you do. But sometimes a man gets mixed up about what's important and what's not. A long time ago I had a woman who loved me the way Jenny loves Drew. We were going to be married. But the war broke out, and I rode off to fight. I thought what I was fighting for was more important. When I finally came to my senses and realized *she* was the most important thing in my life, it was too late. She was gone. And I haven't seen her since."

Curly's chair scraped the floor as he got to his feet and turned to the woodburner, checked on the coffee. He was moved and embarrassed by Torn's words. Torn had bared his soul, and the deputy was for the moment at a loss.

He poured two mugs to the brim with java, and as he put one on the table in front of Torn, he said, "Maybe you should tell Drew about that. Might open his eyes."

Torn nodded pensively. "Maybe I should."

As a rule he did not interfere in other people's lives, but now he tried to persuade himself to break that rule. Before it was too late for Drew and Jenny.

Because, like an animal that could sense bad weather coming, he had a premonition of disaster.

CHAPTER

5

THEY ROLLED INTO ELLSWORTH WITH JENNY SITTING BETWEEN Torn and Curly on the buckboard's seat. She wore a plain gingham dress, and her hair was pinned up beneath a bonnet. Though the dress was somewhat drab and a bit frayed, Torn thought she cut a fine figure. He'd been partial to Jenny from the first time they'd met. The affection he felt for her was almost brotherly. It could not be otherwise in his case. His love for Melony Hancock was too strong—so strong, in fact, that it had survived ten years of futile searching.

Jenny's father had been a horse trader, a worthless boozer who had abandoned his wife and daughter. Her mother, disenchanted with the hardships of frontier life, had gone back east. But Jenny had stayed, being old enough then to make her own way. Torn had met her several years ago in Abilene, where she had been working as a waitress at the Drover's Restaurant. She was kindhearted and uncomplaining, personifying the "good girl" that every mother hoped her son would marry.

Behind them, the morning sun was an orange ball of flame shimmering behind ragged strips of gray cloud. Torn knew that soon enough the clouds would burn away and the sun would rule the sky, turning the prairie into a furnace alleviated only by the ever-present wind, which made the tall grass ripple like a sea of gold.

Ellsworth had prospered since Abilene had closed its doors to the cattle trade. Its burgeoning population consisted of merchants, blacksmiths, saddlers, grocers, gunsmiths, and carpenters, as well as doctors, dentists, teachers, bankers, and lawyers. And then there were those who plied their trade below the dead-line, the gamblers and soiled doves, the confidence men and whiskey peddlers.

Lumber by the trainload was rolling into Ellsworth, and the din of hammers and saws rose from every point as new buildings were hastily raised to house new residents and businesses. A constant haze of dust the color of cornmeal drifted on the wings of the wind.

Torn spent a lot of time in trail towns. They always seemed to produce plenty of work for a circuit judge. He was attuned to the rhythm of life in these wild and wide-open places. He knew that if it survived, Ellsworth would eventually grow tame. The farmers would move in, as they had into Abilene. Before long Ellsworth would realize it could make a living off the grangers—that it didn't need the cowboy anymore. There was a lot of profit in the cattle trade, but it was profit that had a high price. Sometimes, mused Torn, the price was too high. Sam Tucker's death was a case in point.

As they neared the jail they could not fail to notice

the clots of men in the shade of the boardwalks on both sides of the street. Torn could tell by their clothes that they were men from town. They were earnest and unsmiling in their talk, grim and furtive in the way they watched the jail.

"You don't think they'll actually try to take Drew's prisoner, do you?" asked Jenny.

"If they do, they'll be mighty sorry," predicted Curly.

"I doubt if they'll try," said Torn, hoping to quell Jenny's anxiety. "It's one thing to talk about lynching. Doing it is something else entirely. They're angry now, but they'll cool down and see reason."

"Seeing you will throw cold water on 'em," declared Curly. "No call to bring in Judge Lynch when they've got a real judge."

Drew Mitchell stepped out onto the jail's boardwalk as Curly checked the two horses hitched to the buckboard. The Remington scattergun was cradled in the sheriff's arm. He looked relieved when he saw Torn. Still, the smile he bestowed upon Jenny as he held out his free hand to help her down was tight at the corners with stress.

Without a word she wrapped her arms around him and laid her head against his chest, listening with eyes closed to the strong, steady beat of his heart.

"You shouldn't have come," he told her.

"But you knew I would. You sent Curly with the buckboard."

Mitchell looked up at Torn. "You have good timing, Clay."

"Looks that way."

"Poor Sam Tucker," said Jenny. "Why does this kind

of thing have to happen to good people, Drew? Sam never did harm to anyone in his life."

"The cowboy says he didn't mean to kill anybody. He saw Sam charging out of the store with what he thought was a rifle. That's his claim, anyway. Turned out to be an ax handle."

"You believe that?" asked Torn.

Mitchell shrugged. "It was dark, and the cowboy was mad drunk. I don't know. You're the one who has to decide, not me."

"The jury decides."

"The way people around here felt about Sam Tucker, he'd be better off waiving his right to a jury trial. He can do that, right?"

Torn nodded. "He can. Did you tell him so?"

"Not my place to tell him anything. I almost feel sorry for him, though."

"You're not standing up for him, are you?" asked Curly.

"You know better than that," replied Mitchell. "Whether he means to or not, a man's responsible for the wrong he does others."

Jenny reluctantly pulled away from her husband. "I'm going to see if there is anything I can do for Eunice Tucker."

Torn watched her cross the street. Mitchell watched Torn.

"She just seems to get prettier, doesn't she, Clay?"

"You're a lucky man."

"I'm going to be a father. Did she tell you? We've decided that if it's a boy, we'd name him after you. What do you say to that?"

"I don't know what to say. I'm honored."

"You're a good friend, Clay, and a good man. And you know Jenny has always had a soft spot in her heart for you. I confess, I was jealous of you back when we all first met in Abilene. If you'd been so inclined, she might have become Mrs. Torn instead of Mrs. Mitchell."

The light went out of Torn's eyes. Mitchell silently cursed himself. What a fool he was! In his relief to see Torn he'd become too loose-lipped.

Because he knew that if there was ever going to be a Mrs. Torn, her name would be Melony.

Mitchell remembered that Torn carried a photograph of Melony Hancock. When he and Torn had first met, Mitchell had just become Abilene's sheriff, taking the place of the legendary Bear River Smith, whose head had been chopped off by an ax-wielding farmer wanted for murder. Torn had shown Mitchell the daguerreotype and asked if he'd seen the woman in it. Mitchell hadn't, and now he wondered how many hundreds of others had looked at the photograph since and shaken their heads.

"I'm sorry, Clay," he muttered. "I'd have to get smarter to become a half-wit."

"Forget it." Torn forced a smile, but the pain lingered in his eyes.

"Look yonder," said Curly, pointing with his chin at three riders turning onto Main from Kiowa Street.

The trio rode stirrup to stirrup, holding their cowponies to a walk. As Torn watched them coming on he saw Curly lay hand on side gun out of the corner of his eye.

Mitchell saw this as well. "Easy does it," he said.

"They just crossed the dead-line," replied Curly. The

paunchy deputy came across as a shy, agreeable sort, but he wasn't at all shy when it came to a fight, and he wasn't very agreeable with lawbreakers.

"Reckon they have to," said Torn mildly, "to get here."

The dusty, sun-dark Texans checked their horses in front of the jail.

"Name's Shank Hollis," announced the man in the middle. "I'm the Slash-B straw boss, and I've come to talk, not fight."

C H A P T E R

6

Hollis was a lean range rider clad in duster and chaps. His light brown hair was flecked with silver, and Torn figured he was in his mid-thirties—older than most of the cowboys who came up the Chisholm. And wiser, too, hoped Torn, whose first impression of Hollis was that of a man who could be trusted to fight fair if and when the time for fighting came.

"All right," said Mitchell. "But leave your gunbelt hanging on your saddle. Curly, keep an eye on Mr. Hollis's friends."

Hollis swung down, unbuckled his gun rig, and draped it over his saddlehorn. "They won't try anything without my say-so," he promised.

"Just the same," said Mitchell, who thought the young Texas bravos looked about as well behaved as a pair of wild ladino steers.

As Hollis stepped up onto the boardwalk his narrow eyes flicked over Torn. "You the judge?"

"That's right."

Hollis nodded. "Couple of my boys saw you get off the train this morning. Mr. Evans—he's the moneyman who just bought our herd—told me you were expected."

Torn remembered the two cowboys hanging around the railroad station.

"What I got to say," continued Hollis, "you both ought to hear."

"Come inside," said Mitchell, and led the way.

Inside the jail, the sheriff laid his shotgun on the desk. Shank moved toward the two cells in the rear of the long room as Clete came off the bunk in one of them.

"That's close enough," said Mitchell.

Hollis took a long, slow look around. The two strap-iron cells were separated by a short hallway leading to a backdoor that was barred on the inside. The front part of the room contained the desk, a gun case, a washstand, a bunk, and a potbelly stove. The two front windows sported thick shutters with cross-cut gun slots.

"Thinking about trying to break him out?" asked Torn with a humorless smile.

"Hope I don't have to," said Hollis, with surprising frankness.

"That strikes me as a funny thing to say," remarked Mitchell. He didn't look amused.

Hollis threw a thumb in the direction of Clete's cell. "Know who that is?"

"The cowboy who shot and killed a good man, Sam Tucker," replied Mitchell. "He's going to have to answer for it."

"That's Carter Bartlett's son," said Hollis. "Heard of Carter Bartlett?"

"I haven't," said Torn.

"I have," said Mitchell. "A cattleman."

"Not just any ol' cattleman. Next to Captain King, he's got the biggest spread in Texas. He owns Concho County. Clete's his only flesh and blood. Mrs. Bartlett passed on some years ago. So Clete's all Mr. Bartlett's got left."

"Sorry to hear that," said the sheriff.

Hollis glanced at Clete. "You sure got your tail in a wringer now."

"Just get me the hell out of this cage," demanded Clete, surly.

"He's got a wild streak," Hollis told Torn and Mitchell. "He didn't mean to kill that man."

"I don't need you making excuses for me," shouted Clete.

Hollis ignored him. "We just pushed twenty-five hundred head up the trail. Mr. Bartlett put Clete in charge, but he sent me along to keep an eye on the boy."

"I don't need no wet nurse," railed Clete, his fierce Texas pride blazing out of control. "And I ain't no *boy!*"

"You should have kept a closer eye on him," said Mitchell.

Hollis turned to Torn. "No way around this?"

"None that I can see," replied Torn. Torn liked the Slash-B segundo. Hollis seemed like a basically decent man impaled on the horns of a dilemma. He also seemed to be the kind of man you didn't want to tangle with if you could avoid it. He talked straight, and no doubt could shoot even straighter.

"So where does this road lead?"

"He'll have to stand trial," said Torn.

"I've heard about you, Judge. You're the one broke up that Foster-Larkin feud down our way last year."

"They're gonna hang me, Shank!" yelled Clete, yanking on the stout strap iron like a coyote caught in a steel trap.

"Settle down," said Hollis. He exhaled slowly through clenched teeth, and Torn got the impression there was no love lost between the straw boss and Clete Bartlett. "Take your medicine like a man."

"You let them stretch my neck," raged Clete, "my father will shoot you down like a mad dog."

Shank Hollis headed for the door. Torn and Mitchell followed him out. Curly was watching the two Slash-B riders like a hawk. Strapping on his iron, Hollis mounted up.

"You ought to know," he said grimly, "that I sent word to Mr. Bartlett about this."

"Asking for orders," said Torn.

Hollis nodded. "I reckon I know what those orders will be. It ain't a question of right or wrong, Judge. Mr. Bartlett's a good man. He knows Clete's got bad blood in him. But I don't think he can just let Clete hang."

"Sorry to hear that," said Mitchell.

"You and me both," was Shank's heartfelt reply.

Watching the three Texans ride away, Curly let out pent-up breath.

"There's going to be hell to pay," predicted the deputy.

CHAPTER 7

THE SLASH-B CAMP WAS A MILE SOUTHWEST OF ELLSWORTH. The horses and cookfires were kept down in a sandy cutbank draw. At night the men would take their hot rolls up onto the eastern slope of a gentle prairie swell. But during the heat of day they generally dallied around the chuckwagon down in the draw, where tarps had been erected to provide a little shade.

This was where the cowboy called Baylis found Shank Hollis and the nine other members of the trail crew when he rode out from town. It was late afternoon. Uvaldo, the old Mexican who served as the outfit's cook, was transferring an armload of cow chips from the possum-belly slung beneath the wagon to the big cookfire where tonight's supper of son-of-a-gun stew was starting to simmer in a cast-iron Dutch oven.

A glance at the cowboy's horse told Hollis that Baylis had fogged it all the way from town. As Baylis swung down off the sweat-lathered pony the Slash-B segundo stood up. So did everyone else. The boys were bored. They weren't used to being idle. The herd had been sold and they didn't have much to do. Three days and nights on Ellsworth's Texas side had just about cleaned everybody out. Normally by this time they would have been heading home. Hollis knew they were wound up tighter than eight-day clocks. They were past ready to do what they had to about Clete and make for the Red River.

Baylis untied a tin cup from a saddle strap and stopped off at the fire to pour himself a cup of coffee. Uvaldo always kept at least a gallon brewing. A cowboy drank java morning, noon, and night, regardless of whether it was hot enough to boil a man's brains in his head—which was just about how hot this day had become. He watched Uvaldo dump the cow chips on the fire. There wasn't a stick of decent firewood within a hundred miles. As Hollis and the other hands gathered 'round, Uvaldo dumped a few pounds of flour into the oven to thicken the stew, and Baylis made a face.

"I'm sorrier than a wet dog that I don't have enough money left for one more dose of restaurant cooking," he said, sitting on his heels near the fire. "No offense, Uvaldo, but your stew always tastes like you left the hide on, and I cracked a tooth last week on one of your sourdough sinkers."

"You don' have to eat," said Uvaldo, with sublime indifference. "You go ahead and starve to death, and that will be one less gringo I have to cook for."

Baylis grinned, but the grin faded as the shadow of the Slash-B straw boss fell over him.

"I reckon it came," said Hollis.

"Sure enough." Baylis fished the telegram out of a

shirt pocket and handed it up to Shank. "Didn't figure it would, so soon."

"Bad news travels fast," replied Hollis. The Slash B was a thousand miles away as the crow flew, and the wire he'd sent Carter Bartlett night before last had gone roundabout through many keys to get to Rockbottom, the town nearest the ranch. Slash had calculated he wouldn't hear back from Carter before tomorrow at the earliest. He was glad it hadn't taken so long. The whole outfit was slow-burning on a short fuse.

The cowboys bunched around Hollis as he opened the crumpled telegram and studied the terse orders it contained.

> Shank
> Use all the money you need to buy him out. If that does not work, break him out. Do whatever you have to do to keep my boy from the hangman's noose.
>
> Carter

"What does it say, Shank?" asked one of the cowboys.

"Reckon we all know," said Wes Holt. He had been with Clete the night Clete had gotten his tail in a wringer. It was his horse that the sheriff had "borrowed." Holt felt as though he had let Clete down, standing by while Mitchell tossed him in jail, and he was in a hurry to make up for this. Now he pulled his shooting iron out of its holster. He thumbed the loading gate open, put the hammer on half cock, and rolled the cylinder on his arm to make sure there was a bean in every chamber—an action that made it clear to everyone where Holt stood on the matter.

"Put it away, Wes," said Hollis.

Wes scowled, reluctantly obeyed. "Clete's a friend of mine. I don't aim to stand around and do nothing."

Hollis slowly scanned the dark, gaunt faces of the young cowboys. They were all Clete Bartlett's friends. Clete was brash and flashy and dangerous, and they admired him for it. And they were accustomed to solving problems with brawn instead of brains, with scant regard for consequences. Just like Clete.

But Shank was older and, he hoped, wiser. He understood these boys because he'd once been like them. He'd had his wild times and counted himself lucky for having come through them with only a dozen broken bones and a couple of gunshot wounds. These young bravos respected him because he was fair as well as tough. He never asked them to do something he wouldn't do, and he never failed to whip them to a slim frazzle if they failed to follow his orders. But they weren't his friends, and Hollis realized they would obey him only so long as he didn't force them to choose between their respect for him and their loyalty to Clete.

He held up the telegram. "Mr. Bartlett doesn't want trouble if it can be avoided. I guess maybe you haven't thought this thing all the way through to the other side. He has. Clete won't hang. But there's more than one way to skin a cat. We go in making smoke, Mr. Bartlett will have a tough time selling another herd up here. Not just in Ellsworth, but anywhere in Kansas. The word'll get around. And if we can't sell the cattle, we end up without a ranch to work. You boys just remember who you work for. You ride for the Slash-B brand, and that means Carter Bartlett."

The cowboys exchanged sullen looks. Hollis could see his words made sense to them. But they were still as edgy as a passel of painted ladies at a prayer meeting.

"So what are we going to do, Shank?" asked Baylis, rolling a smoke, a muslin pouch of tobacco dangling by its string from his teeth.

"We're going to try the smart play first, before we try gunplay."

"When?" queried another. "I've enjoyed about all this calfin' around I can."

"Yeah, we better not wait too long," warned a rider named Slim. "I know about this Judge Torn. He's as hard and cold as a frozen bullet. Clete don't stand a chance with him."

Hollis nodded. The whole business disgusted him. Personally, he thought the world would be well rid of Clete Bartlett. He wouldn't lose sleep if Clete ended up six feet under. The boy was just plain crazy. Mad-dog mean, too, and not worth the pain of the mother that bore him. Something like this had been bound to happen.

But Shank knew better than to let out how he really felt about Clete. He knew his reasons for feeling this way were suspect. For one thing, he was absolutely devoted to Carter Bartlett. He thought of the old man as the father he'd never had. Shank had wandered onto the Slash B twenty years ago, a wet-behind-the-ears saddle bum without a lick of sense or two red cents to rub together. Carter had taken him in and done right by him every day since. It riled Hollis, the disrespectful way Clete treated his father. In Shank's opinion, Clete didn't deserve the sweat off Carter's brow.

But that wasn't the only source of bad blood between Clete and the Slash-B segundo. There was Caitlin Price. The prettiest girl in Rockbottom. Clete and Hollis had been vying for her attention for quite a while now. It shamed Hollis to think it, but he couldn't help reckoning that with Clete out of the way he'd have clear sailing with Caitlin.

"We'll go in tonight," he told the Slash-B outfit. "If we do it my way, maybe we can get Clete out without any blood-spilling."

Slim shook his head. "Not much chance of that, if you ask me. Not with that tin star and Judge Torn standing against us."

"We could take 'em some of Uvaldo's stew," suggested Baylis, always the jokester. "That would settle their hash."

Some of the others laughed, but the laughter had a grim, harsh edge to it.

"Torn don't worry me," declared Wes Holt, truculent. "If it breathes, it can die."

CHAPTER 8

THAT EVENING, TORN HAD SUPPER AT THE MITCHELL HOUSE. As soon as he was finished eating, Drew strapped on his gunbelt, planted his hat on his head, and kissed Jenny good night.

"You're staying at the jail again?" she asked, dismayed.

"Curly and I both. We take turns walking Kiowa Street. Somebody's got to watch Bartlett."

"You've had prisoners before. You didn't have to watch them around the clock," said Jenny.

Mitchell stared at her. This was as close to petulance as he had ever known Jenny to get. It was so out of character that he was shocked.

"This isn't just any prisoner," he argued. "The man murdered Sam Tucker. Sam had a lot of friends, and they're all worked up. And Bartlett has friends, too, and they're pretty rough characters. Somehow I don't think they'll just stand by and let him swing."

Torn felt sorry for Jenny. It made him uncomfortable bearing witness to what appeared to be the beginning of a domestic squabble. Steeling himself, he jumped into the breach. He couldn't sit by and watch two people he cared about tearing into each other.

"Drew, why don't you let me spell you tonight? Stay home with your wife."

To Torn's surprise, his offer only served to antagonize Mitchell.

"That's not your job. It's mine. If there's going to be trouble, I'm obliged to be where I can stop it. It's what they pay me for."

"Nothing happened yesterday, or all day today. Nothing will happen tonight. Curly and I can handle things."

"I said no," snapped Mitchell. "That's my last word on the matter." Snatching up his Remington scattergun, he started through the door.

"Hold up," said Torn. "I'll walk with you. Give me a minute."

"Make it quick."

Mitchell stepped out, slamming the door. Torn stepped closer to Jenny. She had her apron balled up in both fists and was staring at the door with a stricken expression on her face. Torn pried one of her hands loose from the apron and gave it a reassuring squeeze.

"He's tired, Jenny, that's all. The trial starts tomorrow. I don't figure it will last long. This will all be over soon."

"Will it?" she asked woodenly. "Will it ever be over? As long as Drew wears a badge, this kind of thing will happen."

"Well now, you knew what he was when you married him, didn't you?"

"I thought I could handle it. Now I'm not so sure. It isn't me I'm worried about, Clay. It's our child. You know what I'm most afraid of? Having to tell my son or daughter about their father. What a brave man he was. A good man. 'I'm so sorry you never got to know your father, darling.'"

Her voice cracked with emotion, and she pulled her hand free to wipe furiously at a solitary tear rolling down her cheek.

"I'm sorry," she whispered, forcing a wan smile. "I shouldn't burden you with my silly fears."

"It's no burden. What are friends for?"

She searched his face, looked deep into his slate-gray eyes, and her expression was one he could not fathom.

"I'd better get these dishes done," she said in a small voice, and turned quickly away.

Inexplicably depressed, Torn retrieved hat and gun-belt from the rack near the door. He paused at the threshold to glance back at her. She was busy dumping plates and flatware into a tin basin on the kitchen counter.

"Don't worry, Jenny," he said. "I won't let anything happen to Drew."

As he closed the door Torn realized that was a pledge he would have been better off not making. It was just one of those things people said in such situations, but he was in no position to make ironclad guarantees. He couldn't watch over Mitchell every minute. For one thing, Drew wouldn't stand for it.

Mitchell was waiting out in the road, pacing impatiently. As Torn came off the porch the sheriff bent his steps toward town. He took long strides, but Torn had no problem catching up and falling in alongside.

They walked in silence a moment. The sun had set, leaving the western rim of sky aflame. Ellsworth's buildings stood in stark, black relief against the burnt-orange backdrop. Somewhere across town dogs were quarreling. From Kiowa Street came the tinny sounds of piano and fiddle, and the rumble of cowboy thunder from the dance halls.

"You were pretty hard on her back there," said Torn finally.

"I know. This business with Clete Bartlett's put a bur under my saddle."

Torn didn't know any way to tackle a subject except straight on, so he ducked his chin and waded right in.

"You know, you've got big responsibilities now, Drew. A wife, a child on the way. You ought to start thinking about what's best for them."

"I do. I think about them all the time."

"The job you do may be all right for a single man, but it's hell on a marriage."

Mitchell fired a cross look at Torn. "What are you saying? That I should quit? What would I do for a living? I make a hundred dollars a month. That's a lot of money. Three times a cowboy's wages. It puts food on the table, keeps a roof over our heads. I've never done anything else, and I don't know if I could."

"You could try. What about farming? This is good farm country. Lots of fine land to be had."

"Farming." Mitchell filled the word with contempt. "I was born on a farm. My father broke his back to eke a living out of the land. I watched it make my mother old and gray before her time." Mitchell shook his head adamantly. "I don't want that for Jenny. Or my child."

"There must be more to you than a badge," insisted Torn.

Mitchell rounded on him then. "What about you? If you found Melony tomorrow, would you give up being a judge?"

"I would, Drew, without a second thought. If I had known what was really important in life fifteen years ago, I would have stayed with her and said to hell with the war. But being a judge is a little different from being a sheriff. A lot more sheriffs seem to get themselves killed. That tin star is a target."

"That doesn't bother me."

"I know. But leaving Jenny and your child alone, to fend for themselves, ought to bother you."

By now Mitchell was hot under the collar. "Maybe she'd have been better off marrying you."

"That's a stupid thing to say."

"Why don't you mind your own business?"

"I'm just trying to help."

"I don't need your help."

Mitchell spun on his heel and walked away. Torn watched him go, his anger quick to ebb, then quartered across Main to the hotel.

The fact that he and Drew had butted heads bothered him. He told himself that this was what he got for meddling in the affairs of others. On the other hand, he cared too much for both Drew and Jenny *not* to interfere.

Wrestling with these troubling thoughts, he climbed the hotel stairs to the second-story hall. His room was near the end of the corridor. The hall was dark—the camphine lamps, one at the top of the stairs and the other down at the far end near the window, had not been lighted.

For once his guard was down. He had taken a half-dozen strides before realizing that two men stood in corner shadow on either side of the window. Sweeping his frock coat aside, he reached instinctively for the Colt on his hip. The lethal snicker of a gun being cocked sent an icy chill down his spine.

"Don't do it," rasped a voice he recognized.

Shank Hollis.

The Slash-B straw boss stepped into murky half-light leaking through the window. He held his hands well away from his sides. So it was the other man, realized Torn, who was covering him with a gun.

"We didn't come to trade lead," said Hollis.

Torn rested his hand on the Colt Peacemaker's bone-inlaid handle, but he didn't draw the pistol.

"Glad to hear it," he replied. "So why are you hiding in the dark?"

"Just want to talk."

"You're north of the dead-line and you're heeled," snapped Torn, cutting no slack. "Which means you're lawbreakers."

Hollis refused to be goaded into rash action. "How about it, Judge? Just a few minutes of your time. Maybe we can cut a deal."

"I don't make deals."

"This one might be too good to pass up."

Torn thought it over. He had a pretty good idea what kind of deal Hollis had in mind, and it rankled him that Shank thought he could be bought. But what harm could come of hearing him out? Maybe he could talk some sense into the Slash-B segundo. Hollis seemed like a reasonable man. If there was any way to defuse the situation, Torn wanted to give it a try.

"Okay," he said. "We'll talk."

He took three more steps, which brought him to the door of his room, and face-to-face with Hollis. Now he saw the saddlebags draped over Shank's shoulder. He could also see the second man better. It was one of the cowboys he remembered noticing at the railroad station yesterday morning.

"Tell him to leather his iron," Torn told Hollis.

"Baylis."

The cowboy holstered his gun. Torn unlocked the door, pushed it open, and motioned for Hollis to precede him. Baylis took a step forward.

"No," snapped Torn. "You can wait out here."

Baylis looked to Hollis, who nodded before stepping into the room. Torn entered, shut and locked the door, leaving the key in the lock.

"So how much is there in those saddlebags?" he asked.

Hollis smiled faintly. "You're a smart man."

"Maybe. But one thing I'm not is crooked."

"Well, we sold twenty-five hundred head at eighteen dollars a head. I had to pay the hands and buy supplies for the road home. That left a little less than forty-three thousand dollars. And it's all yours, Judge. Mr. Bartlett says you can have it if you'll just let his son go."

CHAPTER 9

"THAT'S A LOT OF MONEY," SAID TORN, LIGHTING A KEROSENE lamp.

Hollis shrugged the saddlebags off his shoulder, held them out to Torn.

"All you got to do is find Clete innocent. Then you'll be a rich man."

"Problem is, I wouldn't be able to live with myself."

"Hanging Clete won't bring that shopkeeper back."

"You're missing the point."

"No, I'm not. You want to make an example of Clete. Fact is, Clete thought he was defending himself. He thought that man had a rifle, or maybe a scattergun. You know how it is, Judge. From what I've heard, you've been around. If you want to stay alive out here, sometimes you've got to shoot first and fast. You wait long enough to make sure, you might end up shaking hands with Saint Peter."

"He was north of the dead-line, discharging his firearm, in reckless disregard for the safety of others. A man was killed as a result of his actions. That's murder."

"Fancy words. Reckless disregard." Shank smiled dryly. "Yeah, that's Clete in a nutshell. So you won't take the money."

"No."

Hollis draped the saddlebags over his shoulder. "I learned a long time ago that what never bends will break."

"I don't have anything against you, Hollis. You're just Carter Bartlett's messenger boy."

"Carter's a good man."

"You said that once before, as I recall."

"It bears repeating. What would you do if it was your son facing the hangman's noose?"

"If he took the life of an innocent man, I'd kill him myself."

"You *don't* bend, do you?" said the Slash-B segundo admiringly.

Torn walked to the room's only window and looked down the dark, quiet length of Main Street.

"A man by the name of Karl Schmidt took all the bend out of me," he said, his voice only a notch above a whisper. "He was a sergeant-of-the-guard at Point Lookout, a federal prison camp. For sixteen months he tried to break me. I never could figure why he singled me out."

"Probably because he was afraid you were the one man he couldn't break. You were a challenge."

Torn gazed bleakly out at the deepening night, looking across the years at those months of living hell he had somehow endured. It had been a long time ago, but it still seemed like yesterday, so vivid that sometimes he woke up at night with the cold sweats, a hoarse yell dying stillborn in his throat. He was resigned to it always being so.

"Don't try to break Clete out of jail, Hollis," he warned. "I can tell you're loyal to Carter Bartlett, and there's nothing wrong with loyalty—until it leads you down the wrong road."

"I'll be straight with you, Judge. If it was up to me, I'd let you hang Clete and say good riddance. But it's not up to me. And that puts me twixt the post and the pillar. In a way I'm kind of glad you didn't take the money. I respect you for that. In your boots, I hope I'd have the backbone not to, either. So you'll believe me when I tell you I'd hate like double-rectified hell to have to kill you."

Torn turned from the window and looked at the Colt Hollis was aiming at him.

"Looks like I misjudged you," he said, more disappointed than afraid. "You just took your first step down that wrong road."

Hollis was grim as death. He backed to the door and turned the key.

"Baylis!"

The cowboy came in, took one look at the situation, and drew his gun.

"Real slow now, Judge," said Hollis. "Unbuckle that gunbelt with your left hand and let it drop."

Torn gauged his chances. They were nil. He did as he was told.

"Now kick it away."

Torn kicked it away. Did they know about the saber knife? In the past, the fact that he kept it shoulder-rigged under his frock coat, out of sight, had been for him the difference between life and death on more than one occasion. But these days it seemed that more and more people had heard about that one-of-a-kind weapon.

"What are you going to do?" he asked.

"Take Clete home to his father."

Torn's thoughts flew to Mitchell. "You won't do that without a fight. The sheriff in this town doesn't bend, either."

"I don't want any killing," said Hollis fervently.

"I don't either. I especially don't want Sheriff Mitchell killed. He's a friend of mine. He's got a wife, and a kid on the way."

This news made Hollis wince. "I don't have any choice. I can't let Carter Bartlett down. I just can't. I owe him my life."

Torn could see he wasn't going to sway Hollis. The man's mind was made up. Shank was backed into a corner with no way out. Hollis didn't want killing, but Torn could almost smell it coming, and odds were that Drew Mitchell was going to wind up becoming one of the casualties.

"Baylis, you keep a close eye on him," said Hollis. "I reckon he's about twice as dangerous as a hole full of rattlesnakes. Shoot him if you have to."

"You can count on me, Shank."

"Wait," said Torn as Hollis stepped through the door. His voice was sharp-edged with desperation. It was bad enough that Drew was in danger; but when he remembered that he'd as much as given his word to Jenny that he wouldn't let anything happen to Mitchell, he found himself willing to sacrifice justice to protect Drew.

Hollis turned. "Maybe I can trade him these greenbacks for Clete. Then we won't have to trade lead."

"He won't. But let me talk to him."

Hollis quickly considered the offer and discarded it. "It wouldn't do any good, and we both know it."

He went out, closing the door behind him.

Baylis stepped sideways to lock the door. He didn't take his eyes off Torn. He stayed across the room, his back to the wall. A glance told Torn that Baylis would not hesitate to shoot.

"Hope you don't try nothing," said Baylis. "I'd rather not have a price on my head."

Turning his back on the Slash-B cowboy, Torn again checked the street. Five horsemen were emerging from the alley alongside the hotel. One was leading two riderless mounts. They circled around to the front, almost directly below the window of Torn's room. Hollis appeared and climbed into one of the empty saddles.

All five men with Hollis were carrying their rifles in hand. They started down Main Street. Shank gestured for them to fan out. Riding abreast and keeping their horses to a walk, the Slash-B men headed for the jail, which was out of Torn's line of sight.

"Nothing you can do about it, Judge," said Baylis, hoping to nip in the bud any rash action on Torn's part with such confident talk. "It's a sure bet, so don't make a dumb play."

Turning slightly so that Baylis could not detect the movement of his arm, Torn slowly slipped his right hand under his frock coat. A flick of the thumb removed the strap holding his saber knife upside down in its sheath. The weapon fell into his hand.

He didn't think much of his chances. Most cowboys

were at least fair hands with their hoglegs, and some were better than fair. But it just wasn't possible for him to stand by and do nothing.

"You've got me dead to rights," said Torn, working to keep his voice level so as not to give himself away. "What can I do?"

"Not a damn thing," agreed Baylis, sounding relieved. Convinced that Torn was going to be sensible, he relaxed a notch or two.

Torn whirled and threw the saber knife.

THE SABER KNIFE WAS A LONG COUNTRY MILE FROM BEING ANY kind of throwing blade, but long hours of practice had enabled Torn to devise a method that worked fairly well at close range.

Starting down low, he brought his arm up, locked rigid, letting the saber knife go halfway through the ninety-degree arc. Throwing knives were balanced to turn over once every ten feet, but Torn's technique did not turn the saber knife even once. It was simply a matter of hurling the weapon with brute force. Baylis stood about twelve feet away, close enough so that when the saber knife reached him, it still had plenty of velocity.

Torn's aim was deadly. The saber knife struck just above the cowboy's belt buckle. Baylis fired a fraction of a second later. Moving sideways out of his crouch, Torn felt the bullet pluck at his sleeve, creasing his arm above the elbow. It felt like a hot branding iron slapped against his flesh.

With ten inches of cold steel rippling through his guts, one shot was all Baylis was good for. The six-gun slipped out of his hand. Twitchy fingers clutching at the saber knife, he dropped to his knees. Torn reached his own gunbelt and drew the Colt Peacemaker. But Baylis wasn't going to give him any more trouble. The cowboy looked at Torn with an expression of utter disbelief. The breath rattling in his throat, he fell sideways and pulled his knees up. His legs spasmed, and spurs jangled against the floor.

Torn kicked the cowboy's thumb-buster across the room and hastened back to the window. He knocked out a glass pane with the barrel of the Colt and fired two shots at the Slash-B riders in the street below.

Hollis and his men had already pulled up, looking back, their attention drawn by the single shot Baylis had fired. They were quick to answer Torn with a furious volley of rifle fire. Torn dived for the floor as the window disintegrated in a shower of glass shards and wood shrapnel.

He was pretty sure he hadn't hit any of the Slash-B riders, but that hadn't been his first priority. He'd wanted to warn Drew Mitchell, and maybe discourage the cowboys. The Slash-B men were slinging lead at Torn's window as fast as they could work the actions of their repeating rifles. They didn't seem too discouraged, but with what sounded like a full-scale battle being waged in the middle of Main Street, Torn figured Mitchell had been alerted. In fact, everybody in Ellsworth who wasn't deaf or dead had been alerted.

Crawling for the door, Torn reached Baylis as the dying cowboy began vomiting blood.

"I'm sorry," muttered Torn. "You left me no choice."

Baylis stared at him, his eyes sunk deep in bluish sockets. There was neither recognition nor comprehension in them. Torn hated it. Every bit of it. Baylis wasn't a hard case. He was just a cowhand following orders. After years of war, and many more years dispensing frontier justice, Torn had seen a lot of death and done a lot of killing—more killing than he cared to have on his conscience. But in spite of all he had seen, it still bothered him.

Hollis and his men had stopped blasting away at the window, but Torn scarcely noticed. He knew there was only one thing he could do for Baylis. He didn't want to do it, but he felt obliged. Baylis was dying slow. Torn could quicken the end. With a copperish taste in his mouth, Torn grimaced, got a good grip on the saber knife, and pulled it free. An inhuman sound welled up out of the cowboy's throat, chilling Torn to the bone. Blood soaked Baylis's shirtfront, quickly pooled on the floor. He was dead before Torn could stumble out into the hall.

Breaking into a run, Torn listened for more gunfire from the street, heard nothing at all. For a moment he had hope. Maybe Hollis and his men had dusted out, knowing they had lost the element of surprise. Before he could reach the top of the hotel staircase, a sudden flurry of gunshots dashed those hopes. Torn descended the stairs in three reckless leaps. Bolting across the lobby, he heard the deep-throated roar of a shotgun fired full choke and knew it had to be Mitchell's scattergun. The shrill scream of a horse was drowned in another crackling volley of rifle fire.

He burst through the doors of the hotel. His momentum carried him across the boardwalk and into the street, directly into the path of galloping horses. He tried to dodge, was struck a glancing blow, and went into a spinning fall. A gun went off, very close. The muzzle flash momentarily blinded him. The bullet passed so close to his head he thought he could hear it whine. He rolled beneath the hotel boardwalk. Another bullet slapped into the planking above him. And then the horses were past, the thunder of their hooves on the hardpan rapidly diminishing.

Scrambling out from under the boardwalk, Torn got to his feet, looking after the riders, hoping for a shot. They were already out of short-gun range, and a second later they were out of sight as well, swallowed by the night. He turned toward the jail. A horse lay dead in the street. A man lay sprawled in the jail's doorway. Torn could only see the man's legs.

He broke into a run. Reaching the boardwalk, he pulled up short, stunned, feeling as though he had plowed head-on into an invisible wall.

The man who lay in the doorway was Drew Mitchell. Torn knew without a doubt that he was dead.

Someone was running up behind him. Torn whirled, the Colt leveled. It was Curly. The deputy stopped in his tracks, his breathing labored after his sprint along Kiowa Street. When he looked past Torn at Mitchell, he seemed to stop breathing altogether. He shuffled past Torn like a sleepwalker, knelt beside the body. He reached out with a trembling hand and gently shook Mitchell by the shoulder.

"Drew?"

"He's dead," said Torn flatly.

"No." Curly could see as well as Torn that Mitchell had been hit twice, once in the chest and once in the head, but he wasn't prepared to accept the truth. Some truths, Torn thought grimly, were too terrible to accept. He was better equipped to handle terrible truths than Ellsworth's deputy. He'd handled more than his fair share.

Holstering the Peacemaker, he stepped over Mitchell and into the jail. The cells were empty. Clete Bartlett was gone.

"We better get after them," said Curly, his voice dull, his movements listless as he got to his feet. "I'll get a posse together."

"No. You go after them in the dark, a lot of men are likely to get killed. Mostly men in your posse. If you don't lose them, you'll probably ride right into an ambush."

"But we can't just let them get away."

"They won't," said Torn, and those two words were as cold and certain as death itself. "I know exactly where they're going."

And he knew what he had to do.

He was going to bring them all to justice. Clete. Hollis. Every last one of them, even if he had to ride all the way to Texas to get the job done.

Even if he had to ride to hell and back.

CHAPTER

11

WHEN THEY REACHED THE SITE OF THEIR CAMP, SHANK HOLLIS and the Slash-B riders found the old Mexican cook Uvaldo waiting with the chuckwagon packed up and ready to roll. The horses in the hitch had been standing in their traces for quite some time and were stamping and snickering impatiently. Uvaldo was his usual stoic self. He looked as though he could wait until Judgment Day and sail through the Apocalypse.

Which, mused Hollis bitterly, might not be too far off.

The cowboys swung down off lathered ponies and loosened cinches—their hard-run horses needed rest.

"Wonder what happened to Baylis?" asked one cowboy, checking the stretch of night-black prairie over which they had just ridden hell-for-leather.

"Reckon he's dead or worse," answered Hollis, stretching out his spine. He was feeling old and used up all of a sudden.

"Worse than dead?" puzzled the cowboy.

"If he ain't dead, Judge Torn will hang him."

"He didn't do nothing to hang for."

"We all did, tonight. We're accessories to a killing." He rounded on Wes Holt and Clete Bartlett, who stood together near the wagon. If you wanted to find Wes, mused Hollis, all you had to do was locate Clete. Holt followed Clete around like a puppy dog, and Clete seldom failed to take advantage of this misplaced hero worship. Now Clete was using Holt's makings to roll a smoke.

Hollis walked up and slammed Holt against the side of the chuckwagon. Holt struggled, but Hollis pressed harder with a forearm laid across the cowboy's Adam's apple. Holt made strangling noises and quit struggling.

"You had to kill him," rasped Hollis. "You had to gun down the sheriff."

"Ease up, Shank," pleaded one of the other Slash-B hands. "You'll snap his neck."

"I ought to," growled Hollis, but he let go of Holt.

"Damn," muttered Holt hoarsely, rubbing his throat and glaring at the segundo with dark resentment. "What did you expect me to do? He was shooting at us, wasn't he? He killed Casey's horse, didn't he? And put a load of buckshot into Casey's leg."

Hollis turned away, feeling an odd sense of despair. He was wise enough to know that it was the situation he was really angry at. He was just taking that anger out on Holt. If any one person was to blame, it had to be Clete. If Holt hadn't killed the sheriff, someone else would have had to.

But he couldn't shake the feeling that the sheriff had tried to avoid killing anybody. He could have blown

Casey right out of the saddle, but he hadn't. He'd been trying to run them off, and belatedly Shank realized he could have pulled out and told Carter Bartlett that at least they'd tried. That way, he and the boys wouldn't be wanted for murder and Clete would get what he deserved on the gallows.

Too late now.

He walked over to Casey, who was sitting on the ground in among the horses. Casey had ridden double with Slim Taylor, and Slim was hunkered down next to him, pulling off his boot. He poured a shocking amount of blood out of the boot. Uvaldo arrived with a kerosene lantern to throw some light on the situation. The old cook used a skinning knife to cut Casey's blood-slick pant leg up to the thigh. The other cowboys gathered around to watch.

"How are you feeling, Casey?" asked Hollis.

"Well, my toes ain't curled yet," replied the cowboy philosophically, his teeth clenched and cold sweat beading his forehead. He watched Uvaldo cut his pant leg and shook his head morosely. "I sure hated to see that chestnut gelding go down. It was a good horse. Best in my string."

"Double-ought," said Uvaldo, inspecting the holes in Casey's leg. "Someone bring water."

"Here," said Slim, rising to remove a canteen from his saddle. Uvaldo poured its contents on the leg to wash away the blood. Casey hissed through his teeth.

"I count nine holes," announced the old Mexican, dispassionate.

"Dig 'em out and bandage him up. He'll have to ride in the wagon." The Slash-B remuda had been sold along with the herd. Each cowboy had picked one good horse for the ride home.

"What if they get a posse together?" asked Clete, stepping into the mustard-yellow circle of light produced by the lantern. "We can't dally around here."

"What do you suggest?" asked Hollis dryly. "That we leave him?"

Clete scowled. He didn't like the segundo's tone of voice. "Put him in the wagon and let's git."

"That buckshot's got to come out," said Hollis, "and the leg cleaned up. We let it go too long, it might pizen up. Or don't you care?"

"Look here, Shank. . . ."

"No." Hollis took a menacing step, fists clenched, and Clete recoiled, which made Clete even angrier, as he didn't care to show himself for the coward that he was. "You look," rasped Hollis. "That was a dirty deed you pulled back there."

"What? You mean putting a bullet in that bastard's brainpan?" Clete laughed. "Hell, he deserved it, for locking me up in that damned old iron cage."

"He was already dead, Clete. Holt saw to that."

"So what are you bawling about?"

Hollis stared. "You don't get it, do you?"

"Get what?" shouted Clete, irritated by the fact that Hollis was dressing him down in front of the boys. "You're loco, Shank. Plumb loco."

"I must be," muttered Hollis. "When you killed that shopkeeper, I thought, well, maybe it could have happened to any cowboy who'd had a little too much busthead liquor. But when you shoot a dying man right between the eyes . . ." Hollis shook his head. He couldn't find the words to express the full scope of his revulsion.

Clete looked around at the other Slash-B riders, but found no support in their grim-set features.

"Go to hell, Hollis," he growled, and turned on his heel, heading back to the wagon where his sidekick Wes Holt stood.

Hollis returned to Casey's side. Someone had dug out a bottle of whiskey, and the cowboy was nursing on it something fierce while Uvaldo probed to find the first double-ought pellet.

"Save a little," advised Hollis, "to close up those holes in your hide. We ain't got time to build up a fire and heat some iron."

"What are we gonna do now, Shank?" asked Slim Taylor.

Hollis looked at the others. Cowboys were usually as lighthearted as colts in new spring grass. They took adversity with a shrug and a smile. But the Slash-B hands weren't smiling now. They could feel hemp around their necks, and that was nothing to smile about. Hollis sensed they were thinking differently about Clete now. Wondering if Clete had been worth this.

"We ride like hell for Texas," replied the straw boss. "Uvaldo will follow as best he can with the wagon."

"What happens if they catch up with the wagon?" Slim asked, worried.

"I reckon they'll hang me," said Casey, in the laconic way of cowboys everywhere.

"It's Katy bar the door now," admitted Hollis, "and every man for himself. We'll all be papered. The only safe place I know of is the Slash-B range. It'll be better if we split up and try to make it back there on our own stick."

"Maybe there won't be no posse," said one of the hands, but he didn't sound too hopeful.

"If there is one, they won't chase us far," predicted Hollis. "But don't let that feather your bed. There'll be one man who'll come after us all the way and then some."

"Who?" asked Slim.

"The judge."

CHAPTER

12

AT DAYBREAK TORN BORROWED A BAY HORSE FROM AN Ellsworth livery and rode out into the tallgrass. He went as far as the sandy cutbank draw where the Slash-B camp had been. All that remained were the ashes of an old cookfire slowly but surely being scattered by the persistent prairie wind. That, and plenty of sign.

He hadn't expected them to be sitting around having breakfast. For almost an hour he studied the ground, at first down in the draw, then riding a big circle around the site. He took his time and missed nothing. Before long he had a complete picture.

There were eight of them. He recalled seeing five cowboys in the street below his hotel window. Add Shank Hollis and Clete Bartlett to those five, and it meant that one had probably stayed behind in camp last night. Probably the trail-drive cook. But just because he hadn't ridden into Ellsworth and actively participated in the jailbreak did not exonerate the eighth man, in

Torn's opinion. All eight were equally accountable for the death of Drew Mitchell.

Six men had dusted out in the early-morning hours, heading south. Two rode together, the others splitting up immediately after leaving the cutbank draw, striking out on their own. The wagon had rolled south, too. Torn surmised that two men were with the wagon, as none of the six horses appeared to be carrying double.

Finding the splatter of blood on the ground told him that one cowboy had been wounded, and he further concluded that it was the wounded man who was riding in the wagon. They'd sold their strings, and they'd left the horse of the cowboy named Baylis in town, probably somewhere near the hotel. The drift of it all was that the Slash-B boys did not have any remounts, and one man's pony had been killed in the street in front of the jail.

Torn mounted up and rode slowly back toward Ellsworth. He was going to need a good horse to take him all the way down to Texas, and he'd about decided that the bay was good enough to buy outright from the livery. But now he considered finding Baylis's horse and commandeering it. It wouldn't be hard to find. All he had to look for was the Slash-B brand—a mark he was never going to forget.

Taking the pony of the cowboy he'd been forced to kill had much to recommend it. The Slash-B hands would have saved the best horse in their respective strings, and if Baylis's pick had come through three grueling months of cattle push in fine fiddle, then it must surely be a horse to be reckoned with. And it would save Torn from having to purchase the bay. His pay was two dollars a day, and that didn't come with an expense account.

Arriving back in Ellsworth, he found the respectable side of town stirring, while south of the dead-line Kiowa Street looked as dusty and derelict as a ghost town. Dealers and dance-hall queens were sleeping off last night's excesses while the merchants and craftsmen were starting another day of profitable business.

Along Main Street he rode, passing a crowd of the curious gathered around the jail. He didn't look that way. The jail would always remind him of Drew—and of how he had failed his friend. There were such places in every person's life—places he or she sought to avoid at all costs, because the memory of what had transpired there was just too difficult to deal with.

He found Baylis's horse—a leggy buckskin tied up behind the hotel. Torn took it around to the tie rail and water trough in front, checked it over, and gave it the nod of approval. He stared at the "/B" brand and thought, I'm going to bring one of your horses back to you, Mr. Carter Bartlett, and take your son away.

Delivering the bay to the livery, he walked back to the hotel and went up to his room. The cleaning lady was on her hands and knees scrubbing bloodstains off the floor. The room reeked of lye soap—and death. Torn was aware of her watching him as he quickly packed his valise. She seemed to take special interest in his black attire. As he was about to leave she straightened up and brushed a tendril of iron-gray hair out of faded eyes.

"You an undertaker, mister?"

He smiled bleakly.

"In a way," he replied, and moved on.

He was tying the valise and the scabbard containing his Winchester 44/40 repeater to the double-cinch Texas rig on the buckskin when Curly walked up.

"I'd be obliged was you to let me go along, Judge."

"Thanks, but no. You've got to keep a lid on this town, Curly. It's a big job, but you're just the man to do it. Tempers will run high for a spell, after what's happened. Besides, someone needs to look after Jenny."

Curly squinted directly into the rising sun, a red ball of molten fire that seemed to be suspended at the east end of Main Street. He cleared his throat, and Torn could tell that emotion was getting the better of the deputy. He untied the boot containing Baylis's long gun and gave it to Curly.

"What do I do with this?" asked Curly.

"Sell it. Put the money toward burying that cowboy."

"You gonna say good-bye to Jenny, aren't you?"

Torn swung into the saddle. He took a folded piece of paper from his coat pocket and handed it to Curly.

"Here's a letter to my bank in St. Louis. I've got a little money socked away. A few hundred dollars. It's all for Jenny and the child. Don't tell her. Just draw it out and give it to her. A local banker will take care of the transfer."

"Hell, you still ought to say good-bye," persisted Curly. "She'd be hurt if you didn't. Lord knows she's been hurt enough."

"All right," said Torn, reluctant. "Where is she?"

"I took her home. She insisted on seeing Drew's body." Curly winced. "I got to admit, she held up better than I did."

"She's long on courage."

"It's a crying shame," muttered Curly, strangling on

the words. "That's all it is, Judge. Just a damned crying shame. I hope you get 'em all. Every last mother's son."

"I intend to."

With that, Torn reined the horse along Main Street, riding to the Mitchell house on the outskirts of town. Jenny came out on the porch. Torn dismounted, stood there a moment, unsure of himself, unable to find the right words. Tears welled up in her eyes, but she managed to keep them corraled, and also managed that brave smile Torn had come to expect from her.

"I know you're going after them," she said. "I wish you wouldn't, Clay."

"I've got to."

"Is it justice you're after, Clay? Or is it because you feel as though you let Drew down?"

"Not just Drew. I promised you nothing would happen to him."

"You're not responsible."

"I don't agree."

"Drew's dead. You can't bring him back by tracking down and killing those men. Besides, you'll probably be the one who winds up getting killed. For my sake, Clay, don't go."

"I can't let them get away with it," said Torn stubbornly. "I wish I could tell you why. I wish I knew for sure. But I can't just walk away from this kind of thing without trying to make it right, to balance the scales."

"They won't get away with it. They'll answer for what they've done."

"Yes. They'll answer to me."

Jenny had known from the start that to try to dissuade Torn from going after the Slash-B outfit was futile. She came down off the porch and put her arms around him, laid her head on his chest. He wanted to hold her, console her as a friend should, but because his feelings for Jenny ran deeper than just friendship, he was confused, and her embrace, though it was perfectly innocent, made him feel guilty. He held her a moment, awkwardly, and then broke away as gently as possible, turning to swing hastily into the saddle on the buckskin.

"Be careful, Clay," she said. "Come back safe and sound."

"So long, Jenny."

He rode south, across the tallgrass prairie, starting on a thousand miles of vengeance trail.

CHAPTER 13

THE NEXT DAY, ABOUT MIDMORNING, TORN CAUGHT UP WITH the Slash-B chuckwagon. The wagon wasn't moving. It sat out in the middle of the prairie, like a small boat adrift on a sea of grass that seemed to go on forever in every direction.

Torn checked the buckskin on the rim of a prairie swell and studied the situation. He'd expected to overtake the wagon today, but he was surprised to find it like this, with the team still staked out on a picket line and a cookfire going on the downwind side of the wagon. A man was sitting on his heels by the fire. At this distance—a quarter of a mile—Torn could tell very little about him.

Only the one man was visible. Torn was sure that two members of the Slash-B outfit had left the vicinity of Ellsworth in the wagon. Maybe the wounded man was laid up in the wagon itself, out of sight.

The sun was already a blazing demon. The combination of heat and wind could lead to dehydration. It sapped Torn's strength, and he imagined it would be pretty tough on a wounded man. Maybe the gunshot cowboy was unable to travel.

A lot of maybes, thought Torn. He could think of one more.

Maybe it was a trap.

He slowly scanned the prairie, spotted nothing out of the ordinary. But a whole army of men with rifles could hide in the tallgrass. Torn could only hope for the tell-tale flash of sunlight on the breech or barrel of the rifle —if there happened to be one out there somewhere, aimed at him.

The wise course would be to circle, a little reconnaissance. But Torn was in no mood for pussyfooting around. The instincts of a cavalryman were ingrained: ride straight at the enemy. Torn drew the Winchester 44/40 from its saddle scabbard. If a Slash-B bushwhacker was lurking out there in the grass, Torn figured he'd need the long gun to flush the man out.

Knee pressure compelled the responsive buckskin into a ground-eating lope. Torn sat the saddle with a loose, relaxed posture, the Winchester laid across the saddlebow. His keen gray eyes were always moving, checking the prairie, then the wagon and the man by the fire, then the prairie again.

As he drew closer Torn saw a bundle of blankets beneath the chuckwagon. Apparently a man's bedroll, and it looked like there might be a man in it. Torn felt a little better about things now that he thought he'd located the second man. It didn't make much sense for them to arrange a drygulching, since they couldn't know how many men were on their trail. Two men trying to ambush a twenty-man posse was a fool's game if ever there was one. It was more likely that the wounded man simply didn't have the stomach for travel.

The man coaxing the cow-chip fire beneath a blackened iron skillet did not stand up as Torn reached the camp. Torn saw that he was an old Mexican, apparently unarmed. The aroma of beans and blackstrap in the skillet and the fragrance of coffee in an enameled pot triggered growls of complaint from Torn's empty stomach. Though he had bought some beans and coffee and a few airtights of tomatoes and peaches before leaving Ellsworth, he hadn't wasted time on breakfast this morning. And he hadn't felt much like eating yesterday, either. The aromas from the Mexican's fires revived his appetite, which he took as a good sign. But even though it felt like his belt buckle was scraping his backbone, Torn kept his mind on the business at hand.

"Slash B?" he snapped.

Uvaldo nodded, about as expressive as a cigar-store Indian. He methodically stirred the beans and blackstrap with a long wooden spoon.

"Coffee, hombre?"

"You're as calm as a posthole, aren't you? You got a handle?"

"Uvaldo."

"Mine's Torn."

"I know who you are."

"Do you?"

Again Uvaldo nodded. "You are the one Shank said would come."

Torn was trying to keep one eye on the Mexican and the other on the blankets under the wagon. The more he looked at those blankets, the worse the itch between his shoulder blades became.

"Who's that?" he asked.

Uvaldo looked at the blankets, impassive. He didn't answer, just stood up, slow and stiff. Torn covered him with the Winchester.

"If you knew I was coming, you know what I come for," said Torn. "I would've thought you'd be making tracks for the Red River."

"You cannot run away from death when it comes for you, hombre. The best thing for a man to do is not to run at all."

The buckskin snorted and jumped sideways, stiff-legged, as the bullet passed near its head. Torn was almost pitched out of the saddle. A split second later, he heard the rifle's report. The wind tore the sound into fragments. He looked east, saw a wisp of white smoke at the top of a long swell. Smart move on the bush-whacker's part, thought Torn, to put the sun behind him.

He brought the Winchester up against his shoulder and drew a bead on the old Mexican. This was entirely reflex. Kill the closest enemy first. But Uvaldo held his arms away from his sides to indicate that he was un-armed. He didn't appear to be scared. Torn didn't know but that this harmless act might be more treachery. But he hesitated. He'd never gunned down an unarmed man before.

Another gunshot waffled on the wind. The bullet went wide. Torn knew better than to count on the next one doing likewise. He made a decision regarding Uvaldo. Leaving the old Mexican unscathed, he wheeled the buckskin around, kicked it into a jumping-start gallop, and headed straight at the bushwhacker across a hundred yards of gently sloping grass.

The ambusher fired a third time—again his shot went wide. Torn figured he was lucky to be dealing with a cowboy and not a professional gunman. He answered with the Winchester, not really expecting to hit anything firing a rifle from aboard a galloping horse.

The buckskin churned up the slow incline. Torn rolled the Winchester to jack another round into the breech. Cresting the swell, he checked the horse sharply. The buckskin circled, gnashing the bit. Torn searched the tallgrass that brushed his stirrups, looking for a target.

The cowboy popped up into sight a few yards down the far slope. Before he could get off another shot, Torn had fired the Winchester. His bullet sent the cowboy sprawling.

Torn dismounted, worked the Winchester's action again. Hard sunlight flashed off the ejected shell casing. He led the buckskin down the slope. He knew he had hit the man dead center, but he checked just to be on the safe side.

The cowboy lay spread-eagled on his back, dead eyes staring at the brassy sky.

Torn drew a long, ragged breath. Remorse twisted his insides. The cowboy looked very young, and Torn suddenly felt very old. He reminded himself that young or not, the cowboy had been trying to drygulch him. But it didn't help much.

It reminded him of the war. So many young men had died, and in the end it seemed like senseless sacrifice. So did this. Torn couldn't shake the feeling that it all could have been avoided. And that made the deaths of

Drew Mitchell, the storekeeper Tucker, the cowboy Baylis, and now this young drover just that much more tragic.

He climbed back into the saddle and rode back to the chuckwagon. Uvaldo was still standing near the fire.

"Did you kill him, hombre?"

Torn nodded. "It was him or me."

"I told him this would happen. I warned him not to try such a foolish thing." Uvaldo shrugged. "But he was scared. What could I do? I do not tell people how to live, and I will not tell them how to die, either."

"So the bushwhacking wasn't your idea."

Uvaldo returned Torn's steely gaze without flinching. "It was Casey's idea. But I went along. I liked Casey. I like most of the boys who ride for the brand. They are kind of like sons to me. Except that I do not tell them what to do. So you go ahead and shoot me, hombre. I know you are thinking about it."

Torn's smile was cold and thin. "You were supposed to tell me that that bundle of blankets under the wagon was Casey. But you didn't."

"It is better to say nothing if all you can say is a lie. Now, if you are going to shoot me, go ahead. Otherwise, I will take the shovel from the wagon and bury Casey."

Torn slid the Winchester into its scabbard and swung down, ground-hitching the buckskin.

"Go on," he said. "I'll think about it over a cup of coffee."

CHAPTER 14

TORN POURED COFFEE INTO A TIN CUP AND WALKED OVER TO the chuckwagon to make sure Uvaldo came out with a shovel and nothing else. While the old Mexican trudged through the grass to find Casey's corpse, Torn sat on his heels in the shade of the chuckwagon and savored the java.

About an hour later he heard Uvaldo returning to camp and stepped around the wagon to see if the old Mexican had played it smart. Uvaldo was still just carrying the shovel.

"There was a rifle up there," remarked Torn.

"Yes. And a *pistola.*"

"I was wondering if you'd try to use them."

"I am an old man. I don't see too good anymore. But I haven't lost my mind."

Dumping the dregs out of his cup, Torn helped himself to another pour from the coffeepot. "Well, then," he said, "I reckon you'll get a little older."

Uvaldo tossed the shovel into the wagon, washed dirt off his hands with water from the barrel lashed to the side of the cookhouse on wheels. He brought two tin plates and two spoons over to the fire, giving one of each to Torn.

"You're hungry, aren't you?" asked Uvaldo, noticing the surprise on Torn's face. "You might as well eat. I made enough for two. You can have Casey's share."

"You're a strange one," decided Torn. "You sure you know what's going on here?"

"I know." Uvaldo ladled some food onto Torn's plate. "Clete Bartlett killed a man. That doesn't surprise me. Clete has bad blood in him."

"If I remember right, Shank Hollis said the same thing."

"If you ask me, Shank is more of a son to Carter Bartlett than Clete ever has been or will be."

"Where did Clete get this bad blood everybody talks about? Carter?"

"No, hombre. Carter Bartlett is a good man. I should know—I have worked with him for thirty years. I can remember when it was just Carter and me and a couple of other vaqueros, popping the brush for wild cattle to make into the first Slash-B herd. No, Clete reminds me of his mother. She was the only mistake Carter ever made. That woman, she was no good, hombre, I tell you. But what could be done? They say love is blind. She was untrue to Carter, but he always forgave her. Then she died. And now Carter sees her in Clete, and he always forgives Clete all the bad things that boy does."

"He's going to hang," said Torn.

"Maybe. But once he gets home to the Slash B, you will have the devil's own time getting him out of there."

"Then I'll have the devil's own time. No help for it. I doubt if I'll catch him before he gets home." Torn shoveled grub a moment, thinking ahead. "How many men ride for the Slash-B brand?"

"Forty, fifty *brasaderos*. Most of them are good men. Some have been with Carter for a long time. They would do almost anything he asks of them."

"Like kill a federal judge."

"It won't matter what you call yourself, if Carter wants you dead."

"So he thinks he's the law down there?"

"It isn't what he thinks, hombre. It's what everybody thinks."

"What about a sheriff?"

"There is a man in Rockbottom who wears a badge," said Uvaldo, "but he is not much of a sheriff. They say he used to be a real hard man. A Texas Ranger. But sometimes a man loses his courage and cannot find it again. A sad thing to see. You will get no help from him. You will get help from no one when they find out who you are after. It isn't that people like Clete. I don't think anybody likes him. But everybody likes Carter."

"You're helping me, aren't you? By telling me all this? Sharing your chuck?"

A stone wall could not have been less expressive than the old Mexican.

"I won't let any man go hungry if I can help it," he replied. "Friend or enemy, it does not matter. When I was very young, I used to go hungry all the time. Fighting is one thing, starving another. And as for what I am telling you, I say these things because sometimes words can be a greater weapon than a *pistola.*"

"You're trying to talk me into turning back?"

Uvaldo shrugged. "Can you blame me for trying? I don't think you will, but it is worth a try, to save lives. I am old enough to know that living is more important than revenge."

"I'm after justice, not vengeance."

"So you say. But your eyes, hombre, they say something else."

By now Torn had polished off the beans and black-strap. He put down the plate, knocked back the rest of his coffee, and stood.

"Obliged. I reckon I'll move on."

"To Texas."

Torn nodded. "You?"

"*Sí.*"

"Maybe I'll see you down there."

"Maybe," agreed Uvaldo. "But I will reach the *rancho* several days behind you. My guess is you'll be dead by then."

"You're still shooting words at me," said Torn wryly. "If I'm dead, maybe at least you'll see fit to give me a decent burial. Way you talk about folks down there, nobody else in those parts will bother."

"They will do what Carter Bartlett tells them to do. If he wants you strung up in a tree for crow bait, then it will be done."

Torn turned to the buckskin, swung aboard. "I'm sorry I had to kill your friend. But he left me no choice."

"I was wondering," said Uvaldo. "What would you have done if Casey had given up without a fight? You see, he was afraid you would kill him no matter what he did. That is why he tried to ambush you. What do you think, hombre? Would you have killed him anyway?"

"I would have taken you both back to Ellsworth. You didn't ride with the rest of them the other night. But he did, and he would have had to stand trial for his part in the jailbreak and the killing of the sheriff."

"Which is the same thing as killing him. I guess what happened was for the best. Baylis—did you kill him, too? I see you ride his *caballo.*"

"I did."

"How many Slash-B riders are you going to kill?"

"They called it," snapped Torn.

"Adios, hombre."

Torn nodded curtly and rode south. He didn't look back. He wasn't worried about the old Mexican backshooting him. Uvaldo was on Carter Bartlett's side— that much was clear as mother's milk. Which meant he and Torn were enemies. But Uvaldo didn't have to take a chance today.

Because he knew Torn was as good as dead.

Which meant he wasn't going to have to do anything but dig another grave.

CHAPTER 15

NESTLED IN THE *BRASADA* HILLS OF CENTRAL TEXAS, THE TOWN of Rockbottom was a dusty collection of stone, adobe, and picket structures. Most of the buildings lined the town's single street, a wide stretch of rutted hardpan. A few shacks straggled up the rocky flanks of hills speckled with stands of beavertail cactus and an occasional scrub cedar or oak.

Water was a precious commodity in the *brasada,* and Rockbottom owed its existence in large part to Presidio Creek. It wasn't much of a creek—just a trickle of water over limestone, but it was nurtured by year-round springs. Torn's buckskin picked its way carefully across the rocky creek bed, its iron-shod hooves clattering loudly on stone. While the horse drank, Torn leaned forward in the saddle, elbows on saddle horn, and studied the town.

The middle of a summer day in central Texas was a dress rehearsal for hell, and Torn appreciated the speckled shade of the cypress and sycamore trees along Presidio Creek. There didn't seem to be much shade in Rockbottom. Heat shimmered up off the hard-pan of the street and the flat roofs of the stone and adobe buildings. The boardwalks were narrow, uncovered planks rippling like the keys of an old, overworked piano.

There didn't seem to be much going on in Rockbottom, either. An old man sat in the open window of a mercantile, back braced against the frame, sound asleep. A scrawny dog slinked across the street from alley to alley. Torn had been to Texas only once before —the Lone Star State wasn't really his jurisdiction—but he remembered that the siesta was a time-honored tradition Texans had been quick to borrow from their neighbors south of the border. It looked to him like Rockbottom was pursuing the siesta with a vengeance.

To service the cattle spreads in the vicinity was Rockbottom's reason for being. Torn spotted several saloons, a couple of hardware stores, a saddle shop, a barber, a gunsmith, a doctor's office, a livery and wagon yard, a Wells Fargo express office and bank.

He rode in cautiously. It had been just a couple days shy of four weeks since he'd talked to Uvaldo, and he'd had plenty of lonesome trail for riding and ruminating. If what the Slash-B cook said was true, Rockbottom was enemy country as far as Torn was concerned. He wasn't sure what to expect. He'd made good time down from Kansas, but he figured Clete Bartlett, Shank Hollis, and the other Slash-B cowboys he was after had made even better time. He never had a doubt that they would seek to hole up on Slash-B range. It was the safest place for them.

Uvaldo was somewhere behind him, slowed down by the chuckwagon, but Torn would have bet a month's pay that the old Mexican had stopped off at the first telegraph office to send a wire to Carter Bartlett, warning the rancher that Torn was coming.

What would Bartlett do? Torn couldn't be sure. Shank and Uvaldo both had declared he was a good man, but Torn knew that good men could turn bad, and reasonable men could behave rashly, if the situation became desperate enough.

Torn angled the buckskin across the street toward a small adobe sporting a sign that read SHERIFF'S OFFICE & JAIL. As he dismounted, a young woman emerged from an alley between the jail and a mercantile. She carried a wooden tray covered by a square of blue linen. They met at the door to the jail.

She was pretty, her copper-colored hair pulled back in a ponytail, a dash of freckles on her cheeks, skin like alabaster—the kind of skin that burned but seldom tanned. Her eyes were the pale blue of a robin's egg.

Torn swept hat from head and bowed slightly from the waist. Even after many years on the frontier he retained a trace of that old southern chivalry—reflexes that kicked in every time he met a pretty young lady. She was startled by his gallantry. Torn realized he did not cut a very dashing figure. His clothes had about an acre of dust on them, and he hadn't bothered shaving for a couple of days. He looked like a saddle bum, and she hadn't expected a saddle bum to have the manners of a gentleman.

"After you, ma'am," he said, opening the door to the jail and stepping aside.

She thanked him and passed through. He followed

her in. She set the tray down on a cluttered kneehole desk. A man was sprawled on the bunk in one of the cells, sawing logs. The cell door was open. Torn noticed the tin star on the sleeping man's shirt. He also noticed the empty bottle of tequila on the floor beneath the bunk.

"I suppose you are looking for the sheriff," said the young woman. "Well, there he is. Elzy Price. My father. My name is Caitlin."

"Clay Torn, ma'am."

"You're the one, aren't you? The one they said was coming." She looked both curious and a little afraid. "The man who's after Clete and the others."

"Where did you hear that, ma'am?"

"Does it matter? Everybody in Rockbottom's been talking about what will happen when you get here." She stood in the open cell door, gazing pensively at her sleeping father. "I wish you would keep him out of it, Mr. Torn."

"He's the law around these parts, isn't he?"

"He wears the badge. But Carter Bartlett is the law."

"I understood your father used to be a Texas Ranger."

"People change. He sure has. He isn't the man he once was. That doesn't matter to me. I'll always love him. But it matters to a lot of other people. They have this idea about him, and they're disappointed when he falls short of what they expect from him. They like to talk about all his exploits—like the time he rode down Refugio way. A gang of ruffians was making life miserable for the good folks of that town. So they asked the Texas Rangers for help. My father rode in a few days later. The townfolks were pretty upset. They were ex-

pecting at least three or four Rangers. And when the
mayor asked my father why only one Ranger was sent,
my father said because there was only one fight to be
fought."

Torn smiled. "That sounds like Ranger talk."

"What you've come down here to do can't be done.
Oh, you might get a couple of the Slash-B boys before
they get you. But my father can't help you. All you'll
manage to do is get him killed. And I'd rather not have
that happen, if you don't mind."

Torn looked long and thoughtfully at Elzy Price, who
was still passed out on the bunk. Price appeared to be
fit enough for a man in his fifties. He was broad in the
chest and his hands were strong and blunt. His face
was craggy, with a stubborn chin and a nose that had
been broken once. His sandy hair, short-cropped, was
dusted with gray. He looked like a tough customer. But
Torn knew that looks could be deceiving. He had met
tough-looking characters who were short on backbone.
And then there were men like Curly Loomis, the kind
who were easily underestimated, paunchy and gone-to-
seed, but as good as any in a fight, and better than
most.

It was a peculiar situation, and Torn took a moment
to think it all the way through. He admired Caitlin for
her loyalty to her father, her willingness to accept Elzy
Price as he was. She didn't judge him by what he had
once been. That, thought Torn, was true love, and
Torn's first instinct was to have mercy on her. He could
turn around and walk out and try not to involve Elzy
Price at all. That's what Caitlin wanted him to do.

But as he stood there and looked at Price Torn felt a
smoldering anger consume his sympathy for Caitlin

and his pity for Elzy. He could understand how a brave man might loose his nerve. He'd seen plenty of examples of that in the war. But what irked him about Price was that Elzy still wore a badge. He was pretending to be someone he couldn't be. And by so doing he had put himself into the position of corrupting the law he represented. He danced to Carter Bartlett's fiddle. And that was dead wrong.

"I'm sorry, ma'am," said Torn as he stepped into the cell. Bending over Price, he gathered a handful of shirt and shook the man roughly. Price moaned but did not waken. Torn shook him more vigorously and still could not rouse the drunken sheriff.

"Leave him alone," said Caitlin.

"I wish I could," replied Torn, with asperity. "But if he wants to be left alone, he should take off that tin star."

Price was wearing a gunbelt, and Torn drew the pistol from its holster. The gun was an old Walker Colt, a six-shot percussion .44—a relic, like the man who carried it.

"What are you doing?" gasped Caitlin.

Torn put the Walker Colt close to Elzy's head and thumbed the hammer back.

The sound provoked an immediate response from Price. His eyes snapped open, and Torn saw the bright glitter of abject fear in them. Price struggled, but Torn held him down, pressing against his chest, feeling Elzy's heart hammering his hand.

"Be still," snapped Torn.

"Who . . . who are you?" gasped Price.

"Clay Torn. Federal judge."

"Oh Christ."

"Take a message to Carter Bartlett," said Torn. "Tell him he has twenty-four hours to turn Clete, Shank Hollis, and the other cowboys I'm after over to me. You understand?"

Price swallowed hard. "Let go of me," he said, trying to sound menacing. He failed miserably.

"Just do what I told you. Then stay the hell out of my way."

He let go of Price and walked out of the cell, avoiding Caitlin's frosty glare.

"Hey," said Price, his voice shaky. "What about my gun?"

"I'll leave it on your desk, next to dinner."

"He won't do it. Carter won't just give up his son. You're a dead man, Torn."

"We all die," said Torn, turning back with a cold smile. "But I'm luckier than you, Price. I only have to die once."

CHAPTER

16

RIDING OUT TO THE SLASH-B RANCH HOUSE TOOK ELZY PRICE the rest of the day. He'd left Rockbottom in a big hurry, without even taking the time to eat the dinner Caitlin had brought to the jail. Torn's visit had put him off his feed. Now he was sorry he hadn't eaten. Riding in the heat of the afternoon with nothing but tequila in his belly made him feel pretty down in the mouth. Besides, leaving the vittles untouched had been very inconsiderate on his part, after all the trouble his daughter had gone to.

That day, Elzy felt bad about a lot of things. The situation with Clete Bartlett worried him. Now that Torn was here, he was even more worried. Afraid, too, and the fear made him painfully aware of his own shortcomings.

But most of all he felt bad about Caitlin. She was a wonderful person. A man couldn't ask for a better daughter. She was pretty, intelligent, compassionate, and she loved him unreservedly. He wasn't worth it. He didn't warrant all the nice things she did for him. Like bringing his dinner to the jail every day. He was almost always passed out in one of the cells, sleeping off the previous night's excesses.

Elzy knew that seeing him in such a state caused Caitlin a lot of anguish, but she never said anything about it. She never browbeat him or begged him to change his ways. She accepted him for what he was and suffered silently. She didn't throw a tantrum or shed a tear. At least not in his presence. He admired her for that. And he hated himself for putting her through such an ordeal.

Rockbottom was located on the eastern rim of the Slash-B range. The ranch was larger than the state of Rhode Island, they said. To reach the ranch headquarters took six hours of constant riding. Elzy wondered if he could make it. He would have preferred making the trip early in the morning. This time of day, the air was like heat from a fully stoked furnace. It took a toll on Price—seemed to burn the lining of his lungs and sap what little strength he had.

It was the drink, he knew, that made him so weak. He didn't have any stamina. Back in the old days, when he'd been Rangerin', he could take the heat. Hell, he could take anything this country threw at him. Heat, cold, flood and drought, bandit and hostile Comanche. He could ride all day and night and go a week without food or sleep. Now an hour or two of riding took all the starch out of him. Elzy Price was disgusted with himself.

But he couldn't wait till morning to see Carter Bartlett. He wasn't doing this because Torn had given him a message to deliver. He was doing it because Carter had told him to—told him to report to the ranch house the minute Torn showed up in Rockbottom. When Carter told him to jump, Elzy Price asked how high.

That was part of the deal. Elzy sometimes thought of it as a deal with the devil. He was Rockbottom's sheriff because Carter said he could be. If he bucked Carter about any little thing, Carter would replace him with someone else. Oh, there would be an election and all that. But the good folks of Rockbottom would vote for the man Carter Bartlett stood behind. If Carter turned his back on him, Elzy knew everyone else would, too.

He would be out of a job, and it would be downright impossible to find another. No other town would take him on as sheriff. Because most towns needed a real sheriff. Rockbottom didn't. When trouble rode into Rockbottom, Carter took care of it. That was part of the deal, too. Elzy didn't have to do anything. Which was just as well. Last year, three longriders had robbed the express office. Carter and his Slash-B *brasaderos* had tracked the hard cases, caught 'em, hanged 'em, and recovered the stolen loot. Elzy had spent all day drinking tequila in the jail.

That kind of thing didn't happen very often in Rockbottom, these days. Most troublemakers had sense enough to swing a wide loop around Carter Bartlett's range.

This man Torn, mused Price, didn't have much sense.

Or maybe he was just too brave for his own good.

Price could remember what it had been like to have courage. He hadn't given it much thought at the time, of course. To be able to walk into dangerous situations with a smile on his lips and a spring in his step had been something he'd taken for granted. These days he found himself wishing he'd been killed in one of those situations. It would have been better for him and Caitlin and the whole damned world if he had been. Torn had hit the nail on the head with his parting words. A coward died a thousand deaths, a brave man only one.

That very afternoon, Elzy died one of those coward's deaths when a ladino steer broke out of some shinnery as the sheriff approached. Cattle in the *brasada* country actually crawled on their bellies into brush no taller than a man to escape detection, and Elzy was almost on top of the longhorn when it exploded into view, bellowing madly.

Elzy's horse snorted and jumped sideways, and Price lost his seat and toppled out of the saddle. The fall knocked the wind out of him. He groped for his side gun with wheezing sobs. Longhorns were the meanest critters on God's earth. They had killed many a range rider. Elzy got to his feet and yanked the Walker Colt out of its holster. But when he saw the ladino standing twenty feet away, spindly legs splayed and massive head lowered, staring malevolently at him, Price panicked. He started shaking so violently that the Walker slipped out of his sweaty hand. Elzy's knees turned rubbery, and he sat down hard. The longhorn stared at him a moment more, then turned and trotted off.

Price covered his face with his hands. Bitter tears burned his eyes. He sat there for a full five minutes until the shaking subsided. His horse came back and nudged his shoulder with its muzzle. Taking deep, ragged breaths, Elzy got to his feet, staggered, then dropped to his knees and dry-heaved.

In time he found the strength to get up again. He bent to retrieve the Walker Colt. He stood there and looked at the gun in his hand for a moment. He'd carried that gun into many a scrape over the years—had been a Ranger when Captain Sam Walker had persuaded President Polk to order a thousand of these revolvers from Sam Colt to arm the Rangers in their bloody frontier war against the Comanches. The Walker had turned the tide in favor of the Rangers. The six-shooter had been a new concept then, allowing the Rangers to fight from horseback, firing six rounds before having to reload. With a Ranger doing the shooting, the end result was usually six dead Comanches. Elzy had been at the Battle of the Pedernales, back in '44, the first time the Rangers had carried the Walker into a fight with the Indians.

These days a lot of revolvers were more lightweight and more reliable than the Walker. Most of them fired the metallic cartridges. But Elzy had held on to this unwieldy cap'n'ball monster for sentimental reasons. It reminded him of the good old days, before he'd lost his nerve.

The way that yellow dun ladino had jumped out of the brush at him reminded him of that fateful day when he'd stopped being a whole man. The half-breed killer Kiowa Jones had ambushed him just like that. Price had been on Kiowa's trail and the two-legged snake had doubled back and lain in wait. He'd shot Elzy out of the saddle before Price could draw iron. The bullet had struck Elzy high in the chest. He dropped the Walker Colt in the fall. Kiowa had stepped up, grinning like a hungry wolf, and put five more slugs into the helpless Texas Ranger. One in each leg, one in each arm, taking a lot of time between shots, having his fun. The sixth bullet had been in the gut. Kiowa had watched Elzy suffer awhile longer, then ridden away.

Folks said Elzy Price had been lucky that an old Nueces Strip sheepherder named Ortega came along and found him, and luckier still that Ortega had been a *curandero*. They claimed Ortega's herb potions and poultices brought Elzy back from death's door. Price had long since concluded that he hadn't been lucky at all—that it would have been better to die in the blood-blackened dust of the ambush site.

Because ever since then he'd been a yellow-bellied coward.

Standing there in the hot sun, feeling sick and humiliated and full of self-contempt, Elzy Price decided it would be better for everybody if he just ended it all.

With that in mind, he cocked the Walker Colt and put the barrel to his head.

He squeezed his eyes shut and tried to pull the trigger.

But he couldn't. He started to shake all over again. He broke out in a cold sweat. He felt like throwing up. He cursed himself, loudly and bitterly.

Gagging on self-disgust, he shoved the Walker into its holster, caught up his horse, and rode for the Slash-B ranch headquarters.

He told himself that with Torn here there would be plenty of killing. Maybe, when the shooting started, he would catch a bullet.

It would be in the back, of course. Because he'd be running away.

CHAPTER 17

THE BARTLETT RANCH HOUSE STOOD ON HIGH GROUND AND looked like a fortress strong. Indeed, in the old days, it had withstood the attacks of Comanche war parties as well as the bandit armies that had once roamed the *brasada*.

It was a large, square, one-story structure, flat-roofed, encircling a vast courtyard. On the east and west sides were heavy-timbered carriage doors, reinforced with strap iron. These opened into passages through which wagons and livestock could be driven into the protection of the courtyard. Two wells provided plenty of water.

Thick shutters with gun slots could be closed over the long narrow windows in the exterior walls. A four-foot adobe palisade along the outer rim provided cover for men positioned on the roof. A wide gallery with broad stone arches shaded the windows and doors all around.

Bunkhouses, barns, corrals, and a host of outbuildings encircled the house. There was plenty of activity even though the day was drawing to a close. A dozen Slash-B hands were breaking horses in two of the corrals. Pale dust rose against the purple sky. Price spotted a couple of lookouts on the roof, silhouetted against the sunset. Before he could get within two hundred yards of the place, two riders galloped out to intercept him.

One was Shank Hollis. The segundo anxiously searched Elzy's face.

"He's here, ain't he?" asked Hollis, his voice hollow.

Price nodded. "Afraid so."

Hollis turned to the other rider. "Go tell Mr. Bartlett it's the sheriff."

The cowboy hurrahed his pony on back to the house. Hollis rode along with Price, stirrup to stirrup. He looked downright glum, and for a moment they shared a morose silence.

"I guess I knew he would," said Hollis finally. "I seen it the first time I laid eyes on the man."

"The kind who keeps on coming on?" said Price.

Hollis nodded. "That kind."

"The law has a long arm."

"It's all Clete's fault," muttered Hollis darkly. "Somebody should have put a bullet in that boy a long time ago. We'd all be better off."

This surprised Price. Not that Shank felt that way, but that the Slash-B foreman would actually air his feelings.

"How's Caitlin, Mr. Price?"

"She's fine, Shank."

"I wish—" Hollis cut himself short with a fierce shake of the head.

Elzy felt sorry for him. He knew Hollis was sweet on Caitlin. Price didn't object. He thought Shank was a pretty good man. A long sight better than his daughter's other suitor—Clete Bartlett. Price guessed that Hollis was wishing he knew if he had a chance with Caitlin. That was a question Price didn't have an answer for. He wasn't sure how Caitlin felt about the two men who were vying for her affection. She never talked to him about it. He thought she liked both Shank and Clete, which was something Price couldn't understand. The two men were as different as night and day. Shank Hollis was soft-spoken, hardworking, reliable. Clete, on the other hand, was a wild, dangerous no-account. Perhaps each man appealed to a different side of Caitlin.

Carter Bartlett was waiting for them in the big room with the walk-in fireplace large enough that whole trees were burned in it. Above the mantel—a twelve-by-twelve timber almost thirty feet long—was a mounted set of longhorn headgear, the biggest set of horns Price had ever laid eyes on. They made the horns on the dun ladino he had run into earlier that day look like toothpicks. The room itself was big enough to hold a square dance in.

That was Carter's style, mused Price. He wanted what he owned to be the biggest and the best, even if it wasn't practical. Take the fireplace, for instance. Winter in the *brasada* hills got cold, sure, but it was never cold for extended periods, and some years there wasn't enough snow to stick to the ground. Still, Carter had to have a fireplace that looked like it belonged in some medieval castle.

When Price walked in, Carter came across to shake his hand. Bartlett looked like a man carved out of a chunk of granite. He was as thick through the body as he was wide. His blunt-fingered hands were as big as skillets and just as strong, his skin brown and tough like old saddle leather. A shock of unruly white hair was brushed straight back, long enough to curl over the collar of his shirt. He was a brawny, vigorous man with piercing eyes, booming voice, and a forceful personality.

"Hello, Price," he said, with a perfunctory smile. "Thanks for coming."

Like I had a choice, thought Elzy.

"Reckon I know why you're here," said Carter.

"He rode in today, Mr. Bartlett."

Carter turned, motioned at the three cowboys ranged around the room. "You know Slim Taylor, Billy Sheen, and Mace Fletcher. We're waiting on Clete. I sent Wes Holt to fetch him."

Price nodded at the Slash-B riders. "You boys look mighty solemn. You must be the ones he's come for."

"They are," said Carter. "How about something to cut the dust, Price?"

"Sure," said Elzy, trying not to sound too eager. He followed Carter to a long sideboard and waited impatiently while Bartlett poured him a glass of bonded liquor. Elzy's mouth started to water when he saw the label on the bottle. Top-of-the-line sippin' whiskey. But he downed it in one gulp. Liquid fire spread through him and smoothed out the rough edges of jangled nerves.

"So how do you read him?" asked Carter.

"Who? Torn?" Price grimaced. "His being here says enough, doesn't it?"

"I was hoping—" Carter stopped, shook his head, smiling ruefully. "When Uvaldo sent the wire, I told the boys here it was too early to start sweating. A lot of things could happen. Why worry till he showed? He might turn back. He might get bushwhacked by outlaws on the trail. He might fall in a damned river and drown. We didn't have to cross this bridge till we come to it. Well, I reckon we come to it now."

"So what do we do, Mr. Bartlett?" asked Slim Taylor. "I don't hanker after going back to Kansas to hang."

"You won't hang," promised Carter gruffly.

Clete and Wes Holt arrived. Clete sauntered across to the sideboard, slapping his leg with the quirt dangling from his wrist. He poured himself a long drink and leered crookedly at Price.

"Hello, Sheriff. Been in any gunfights lately?"

Wes Holt snickered.

"Shut up, Clete," barked Carter.

Price smiled tightly. "That's okay, Mr. Bartlett."

Clete knocked back the liquid bravemaker, slammed the glass down on the sideboard, and hitched at his gunbelt. "So the sonuvabitch is finally here. Good. I'm tired of waitin'. Let's ride in and finish it, once and for all."

"He's a federal judge," said Shank Hollis.

"I don't give a damn," said Clete, truculent.

"That's your problem," said Carter. "You don't give a damn about anything, except yourself."

Clete was startled. He wasn't used to his father talking that way to him. "You got no call to say such to me."

Carter's eyes flashed with anger. "I should never

have put you in charge of that cattle push, boy. I knew it was a mistake. But I was hoping you'd learn something about responsibility. Besides, I needed to stay here, what with those night riders over in the Concho Breaks giving us trouble." Carter drew a deep, calming breath, turned back to Price. "What did this judge say to you, Elzy?"

"He said to tell you you had twenty-four hours to turn Clete, Shank, and these others over to him."

"He has a lot of gall," exclaimed Wes Holt, offended. "Riding into this country and telling you what to do, Mr. Bartlett. One man alone."

"One man, one fight," muttered Price, but nobody was listening to him anymore.

Carter pulled on his chin. "I want you boys to know that I'm not going to let him haul you back to Kansas. What you did, you did on my orders." He fired a sharp look at Clete. "You're responsible. You're the one who gunned down that shopkeeper."

"It was an accident, Pa," said Clete, apprehensive, and putting on a meek act.

"I know. We all make mistakes."

"Is that what you plan to tell Torn?" asked Price. "If so, I think you can save your breath."

"I'm going to chew the breeze with him." Carter nodded. "Reckon I best take the measure of this man myself. Now, you boys listen good. For the time being, you swing wide around Rockbottom. Goes for you, too, Clete."

"Hell, no," said Clete. "I ain't seen Caitlin for a long time." He grinned at Price. "How is my little darlin'? I guess she talks about me all the time, don't she?"

Elzy shot a quick glance at Shank Hollis. The Slash-B

foreman was watching Clete the way a dog with a bone watches another dog that has come a little too close.

Carter stabbed Clete in the chest with a finger. "You'll stay away from Rockbottom like I said, boy. Don't buck me on this. I've given you way too much rope over the years. I see that now." He turned to Price. "You're welcome to stay over, Elzy."

"Thanks," said Price, grateful. Carter always treated him with respect—more respect than he thought he deserved. Carter was a good man. "But I think I'll go back tonight."

"Fine. If you see Torn, tell him I'll be riding in tomorrow morning to palaver."

"I'll tell him," said Price, turning to go. "But I don't think he come all this way to talk."

CHAPTER 18

WHEN TORN CAME OUT OF ROCKBOTTOM'S ONLY HOTEL EARLY the next morning, he found a couple of men standing around out front. They stopped talking to each other as soon as he appeared, and fastened unfriendly eyes on him as he passed. Both were dressed like town dwellers. Torn didn't see any guns, but one was wearing a broadcloth coat buttoned up, so there was no way to know for certain whether he was heeled.

A woman stepped out of a general store and passed Torn. She carried a wicker basket containing several airtights and a loaf of bread. He touched the brim of his hat, smiled politely, and said good morning. She avoided him like the plague. Torn shrugged and walked on, aware that the two men who had been standing in front of the hotel were now following at a discreet distance.

He stopped off at the barbershop to get a trim and a shave. The barber's hands were shaking, so when time came for whisker scraping, Torn wondered if he was going to get his throat accidentally cut. He decided it would be prudent to do the job himself. The barber started to object, but a frosty glance from Torn and the objection died stillborn.

Emerging from the barbershop, Torn saw that a third man had joined his two shadows. He ignored the trio and quartered across the street to the Oriental Restaurant. It was here, at a table by the window, that Elzy Price found him.

"Join me for breakfast, Sheriff?" asked Torn.

The civil offer startled Price. "Uh, no, thanks just the same."

Elzy didn't feel much like eating. This was the first time in months he'd been up and around so early, and it made him feel queasy. He needed a drink, bad.

"Is there a law in this town against loitering?" asked Torn.

"Why?"

Torn nodded out the window. The three men stood in front of the express office directly across the street, watching the Oriental. They reminded Torn of three buzzards on a tree limb, waiting for something on the ground to die.

"Rockbottom's welcoming committee?" he queried.

Price studied the trio. "I'll have a word with them. You should understand, Torn, folks around here like Carter Bartlett. Almost all of them are obliged to him, one way or another. Couple years ago, a twister blew through here and smashed Blodgett's dry-goods store into so much kindling. Carter helped him start all over again. When Maude Phelan's husband died, Carter gave her enough money to get back to her folks in New Orleans. People don't forget those kind of doin's."

"What's that got to do with me?"

"They figure you come to hurt Carter. That makes 'em angry. The whole town stands against you."

"Including you?"

"Carter gave me this job when nobody else would give me the time of day."

Torn's breakfast came: eggs, bacon, biscuits, and grits.

"You don't think they'd lace this with strychnine, do you?" he asked Price, only half kidding.

Price had to smile at that. "Another time, another place, I could get to like you, Torn."

"I've heard about you," said Torn. "They say you could walk 'em down. What happened? How did you get into this?"

"Into what?" Price was defensive, no longer smiling.

"Into Carter Bartlett's pocket."

"None of your business," snapped Price.

Torn nodded. "You deliver my message?"

"Yeah. Carter's riding in this morning. He wants to talk."

"There's nothing to talk about."

Price stood up, exasperated. "You're a gold-plated fool, Torn, for coming here. You can't win."

"The law always wins, sooner or later. I'm surprised you don't know that."

Price left him. Torn watched him cross the street and pass a few words with the three men in front of the express office. The sheriff walked on. The three men stayed.

Torn took his time over breakfast, thinking over

what Elzy Price had said. So Carter Bartlett was a good man. Didn't seem to be any denying that. Too bad for him, then, that his son had bad blood. Drew Mitchell lay cold in the ground because of Clete, and Torn wasn't going to let that deed go unpunished, or the killing of the Ellsworth shopkeeper Tucker.

Breakfast finished, he stepped out into the street. The sun had risen above the hills, and the day was heating up. He had given Bartlett twenty-four hours to deliver Clete and the others into his custody. There were a few hours remaining in that ultimatum. He decided to return to his hotel room. He'd clean his guns and wait for Carter Bartlett. No harm in hearing the man out. Torn just hoped he had better sense than to try a bribe.

He angled across the street. The three men fell in behind him. Torn was becoming increasingly aggravated. He stopped, turned, gave them a hard stare. They stopped, too, but they didn't back off. Torn was of a mind to confront them, pick a fight. But he thought better of it. His quarrel wasn't with the good people of Rockbottom.

He walked on. A man stepped out of the general store, a new cigar clenched in his teeth.

"Got a light, mister?"

"No," said Torn. He tried to go around, but the man sidestepped to block him off.

"Stranger here, aren't you?"

"You taking a poll?" asked Torn dryly.

He glanced over his shoulder. The three men who had tailed him now quickened their pace to close in from behind.

Torn lashed out, grabbing the man in front by the

lapels of his brown broadcloth and spinning to hurl him bodily into the other three. Two of the men went down in a cursing tangle. The other two moved in. Torn drew the Colt Peacemaker.

"I'm in no mood for this," he warned.

A whisper of sound made him turn. Two more men were rushing out of the alley between the general store and the hotel. One was wielding an ax handle, which he swung at Torn's head. Torn ducked under the vicious swing. The ax handle smashed the general store's plate-glass window. Torn plowed into the man, hitting him in the chest with a shoulder, knocking him down.

The second man threw a punch, striking Torn a glancing blow. Someone else slammed into him from behind, hammering him into the front wall of the shebang. One of his assailants tried to wrestle the Colt out of his grasp while the others pounded him with their fists, cursing him with every blow.

Torn managed to keep possession of the Colt. He made a snap decision not to use the gun. These men didn't seem to be armed. They intended to beat him into a bloody pulp with their fists. Torn couldn't bring himself to shoot unless he was shot at.

He fought like a wildcat, smashing one man in the face with his fist, laying the Colt's barrel across the skull of a second, dropping him. The others swarmed, raining blows. Torn's knees buckled and he went down, fighting all the way.

A shot rang out.

Torn blinked blood out of his eyes and looked up to see his attackers backing off. All except the one he'd pistol-whipped—that one was sprawled unconscious on the boardwalk.

In the street was a big man on a big sorrel horse. He was pointing his six-gun skyward. Smoke trickled out of the barrel.

"What the hell's going on here?" he barked.

"Mr. Bartlett!" gasped one of the men, winded, wiping blood from a cut lip. "We were just . . . we just thought we'd . . ."

"Hardeman, if brains were bullets, you'd be plumb out of ammunition," was Carter Bartlett's scathing retort. "Six to one. Odds good enough for you?"

Stung by the reproach in Carter's booming voice, the men exchanged sheepish looks. Torn got unsteadily to his feet.

"You boys go on," said Bartlett. "I appreciate what you all are trying to do for me, but you're just making it worse. Now move."

They drifted away, hangdog. Torn holstered the Colt Peacemaker.

"Your name Torn?"

"That's right."

"I'm Carter Bartlett."

"Figured as much."

Carter holstered his gun, swung down out of his hand-tooled saddle, and tied the sorrel's reins to a shaggy cedar tie rail.

"Why didn't you use that hogleg, Mr. Torn?"

"No need. We were just having a friendly misunderstanding."

Bartlett knelt and checked the unconscious man. "Seth Lockley. Works at the freight company. You rang his bell. But he'll come around."

"You've got a lot of friends around here, Mr. Bartlett."

"You can't say the same, Mr. Torn."

They stood there a moment, sizing each other up. Carter was twenty years older, but Torn decided he didn't want to have to tangle with this man unless it became absolutely necessary.

Bartlett thumbed over his shoulder at the Southern Saloon. "I want to talk to you. How about some tongue oil? Then we'll cuss and discuss, as they say."

Torn nodded. "Don't mind if I do. Beats getting your head bashed in, any day."

CHAPTER 19

Torn THOUGHT IT WAS A LITTLE EARLY FOR A DRINK, UNDER normal circumstances, but he couldn't think of anything better than good whiskey for calming the nerves and washing the copper taste of blood out of his mouth.

The Southern Saloon was like a hundred others he had seen, a long, narrow room with a pier glass behind the mahogany, a high green tin ceiling, a half-dozen deal tables and a faro rig in the back. A man was swamping the place out, and another stood behind the bar, polishing shot glasses with his canvas apron. Both men froze when they saw Torn and Bartlett enter the establishment. Their eyes widened. The barkeep's jaw got slack. Torn figured they were wondering if he and Carter were fixing to square off. They looked mighty nervous.

"Relax, Ben," said Bartlett as he and Torn bellied up to the long, scarred mahogany. "We come in here to play some chin music, not trade lead."

107

The bartender started breathing again. "The usual, Mr. Bartlett?"

Carter nodded. The barkeep produced a bottle of Kentucky bourbon.

"Will this do?" Carter asked Torn.

Torn was smiling. "By God, yes. Is it the real thing?"

"Damn well better be," growled Carter. "I bought a whole case and paid to have it shipped all the way out here."

The bartender provided two shot glasses. Carter poured. Torn sipped, and his smile broadened.

"Ain't rotgut, is it?" asked Carter.

"No indeed."

Carter knocked his drink back and poured himself another. He topped off Torn's glass.

"Ben, you reckon Mr. Torn and I could talk privately?"

"Sure, Mr. Bartlett."

The barkeep circled the mahogany and spoke to the swamper. Both men headed for the back.

"Everybody in town do what you tell them?" asked Torn.

"If so, they do it because they want to. I don't hold a gun to their heads."

"No, not a gun. Money. Every saloon owner and shopkeeper in Rockbottom knows you can make or break him."

"You won't hear anybody complaining."

"They wouldn't take the chance."

"Why don't you go back where you came from, Torn, and stop muddying up our water?"

"I will. But when I go back, I'll be taking your son with me."

"I've got a proposition for you."

"You already tried to buy me once. I hope you don't make the same mistake twice."

"I never do. That's not what I mean. That money I got for the sale of the herd—I'll give it to the widow of the man Clete shot. You can have it now. We'll walk over to the bank. You can ride out of here today. She'll be set for the rest of her life. What do you say?"

"What about the widow of the sheriff your men gunned down breaking Clete out of jail?"

"I wasn't told he had a wife. Split it between them."

"That sheriff happened to be a friend of mine," said Torn coldly.

"So it's revenge you're after. Be sensible, man. Wouldn't those women be better off if you took the money? What good will my son's death do them?"

Torn refrained from a quick refusal. He forced himself to consider the offer carefully. His first inclination was to turn it down flat. But this was a lot of money they were talking about. Jenny Mitchell and her child would be well provided for. It offended his sense of justice, but he couldn't deny that Bartlett had a legitimate point. Justice wouldn't keep a roof over Jenny's head or food on her table. It wouldn't bring Drew back.

It was a tough decision. Torn wavered. That, he mused, was what cold, hard reality did to high ideals. What made it doubly difficult was the fact that he wasn't dealing with hardened criminals here. With the exception of Clete, he was dealing with men who were basically decent. Justice was easier to swallow when he wielded it against ruthless outlaws.

"Bad business from the start," said Bartlett, with sincere regret. "If anyone's to blame, it's me. I shouldn't

have put Clete in charge of that drive. I was hoping
. . . well, it doesn't matter now. If it's blood you want,
Torn, take mine. I'm responsible. I'm the one who told
Shank Hollis and the boys to break Clete out of jail. If
you're bound and determined to take someone back,
take me. You can have the money, too. Just leave my
boy alone."

Torn drew a long breath, shook his head. "I can't."

"You mean you won't," rasped Carter. "By God,
you're as thickheaded as a government mule. I'm trying to stop the killing, damn it. But you're just too
damned proud to back off, aren't you?"

Torn downed the rest of his bourbon, felt the whiskey's heat spread through his body and smooth out the
edges. This time Bartlett made no move to replenish
his glass.

"Clete and the others broke the law," he said flatly.
"They've got to pay the price. No one else can pay it for
them. It just doesn't work that way."

Bartlett removed his hat, set it on the bar, and ran
gloved fingers through his shock of white hair. He was
agitated, and trying his best to stay calm.

"You just don't see. I've invested a lifetime of sweat
and blood into the Slash B. For all his shortcomings,
Clete's all I have. He's the only one I can leave it all to.
Without someone to leave it to, all my work—all my life
—has been for nothing. But you don't savvy, do you?
You don't know what it means to build something like
the Slash B. You don't know what family means, either."

"No," said Torn. "All that was taken away from me.
All I've got now is the law. And if I take your money and
ride away, then I don't even have that."

Carter finished his drink. He was trembling. Spinning, he hurled the empty shot glass across the room. It bounced off the far wall without breaking, rolled under one of the deal tables. Torn didn't flinch, didn't move. He watched Bartlett the way a man watches a coiled rattlesnake.

Breathing raggedly, Carter slowly turned to face him. He had his head down, his fists clenched. His gimlet eyes bored straight through Torn.

"I'm of a mind to finish it right here."

Torn nodded. "You could. I'd be dead one way or the other, I reckon. Either you shot me down, or the good folks of Rockbottom would likely hang me for killing you."

Carter stood there for what seemed to Torn like a small eternity. Torn realized he did not want to shoot this man. The situation was getting out of hand. It had been getting out of hand since the moment Clete Bartlett had shot that Ellsworth shopkeeper down in the street. One thing led to another, one death to another, and there didn't seem to be any stopping this avalanche of violence.

Then Carter unclenched his fists. His breathing leveled out. "No," he said. "No, I don't want killing. That's what I'm trying to step around."

"Then hand over Clete and the others."

"I can't do that. You'll never find them, Torn. The Slash B covers a lot of country. If I don't want you to find them, you won't. And I'm giving you fair warning, here and now. You're not welcome on my property. You cross the line, you'll be trespassing. There'll be fifty cowboys roaming the *brasada* with orders to shoot you on sight, and they'll be within their rights to do so."

Bartlett grabbed his hat and headed for the sun-hammered street. He paused at the door, looked back.

"Have another drink. It's on me. And stay the hell off my range."

After Bartlett had gone, Torn poured himself another shot of bourbon.

CHAPTER

20

Early next morning Torn set out for the Slash-B range. Nobody in town would tell him how to get to the ranch headquarters. He asked the desk clerk on his way out of the hotel. He asked the storekeeper as he bought provisions for a week in the *brasada*. He asked the blacksmith at the livery. He got a blank stare from the first, a hostile look from the second, and a curt "Hell no" from the third.

He had to saddle the buckskin himself. Apparently no one in Rockbottom was the least bit inclined to lend him a helping hand. He rode due west out of town. There was no road to follow, no sign to guide him, but he knew the Slash B was west, and he figured he would just ride until he ran up on something.

His options were few, his chances bleak.

He could sit tight in Rockbottom, hoping one of the men he was after would be foolish enough to show his face, but that had all the makings of a long, unpleasant, and ultimately fruitless vigil. The good people of Rockbottom might get used to his hanging around, or they might just get fed up with it. He didn't want to have to start killing people just because he wasn't welcome, so he decided against this option. Besides, he was by nature a man of action, and idly waiting for something to happen was not his long suit.

Combing the Slash-B range did not promise to be any more productive. No doubt Carter had spoken true words about his chances of finding Clete and the others if they did not wish to be found. There were a thousand places to hide in these hills. Or Carter could just keep his son corralled at the ranch headquarters and protect him with half a hundred cowboys with loaded guns and orders to shoot. Torn had faced tall odds before, but never that tall.

Still, he had to make an effort, and hang the odds. He was committed to bringing Clete, Shank, and the other cowboys who had been in Ellsworth to justice, and he couldn't bring himself to give up on the task, impossible or not. He wasn't a quitter.

So out into the *brasada* he rode, and he rode all day without seeing a living soul. That night he camped under the stars and listened to coyotes serenade the moon. He built a big, crackling fire, hoping to attract trouble of the Slash-B variety. At least that would be a start.

He pictured himself roaming the range for days, even weeks. Maybe he could play and win a game of nerves. If they knew he wasn't going to give up and go away, maybe they would come out and face him, just to end it one way or the other. Admittedly, not a very practical plan for a man alone to pursue. But what else was there?

No one came calling that night, and the next day Torn kept riding. He cut the sign of several riders on shod ponies. It was old sign, but he followed it north by west just the same. Midday came and went and he still hadn't found anyone, and he was beginning to wonder if he ever would. The Slash B was a big ranch indeed.

Late that day he found water, the first since leaving Rockbottom. By *brasada* standards it was a rip-roaring creek. Anywhere else it would have been just a serpentine trickle of spring water through a wide, rocky bed. Cypress trees provided good shade. Torn decided to make an early camp. The buckskin needed rest. Traveling through the brush was hard on man and beast. Circling impenetrable clumps of black jack and beavertail, a rider had to cover two miles worth of ground to make one mile of distance. Horse crippler and cholla lurked in the dry brown grass, threats to lame a pony. Backbones of limestone and deep, rocky draws presented more obstacles, making crossing the *brasada* even more rigorous.

Torn hobbled the buckskin and built a good fire. He propped his saddle between cypress knees and made himself comfortable, eating peach halves in syrup from one airtight while a can of beans heated up. The sun sank below the western rim and the earth cooled. He spotted whitetail deer off in the distance, warily coming down to the creek to drink. In the tree above him, a mockingbird sang his last song of the day to the deepening twilight. After the endless monotony of the scrub, this stand of cypress was pleasing to the eye, and for the first time in a long time Torn relaxed.

As the indigo shadows of night came creeping through the trees and the first stars winked at him from a darkening sky, his thoughts strayed, as they often did in those rare moments of peaceful solitude, to Melony Hancock. He took the daguerreotype from the inside pocket of his black frock coat and gazed with bitter-sweet recollections at the faded image of the woman he had loved and lost and searched for all these years. He wondered what she was doing at this very moment, and if she ever thought of him.

He knew that someday he would find her—he refused to think otherwise. He promised himself that when that day came, when finally they were together again, he would leave the pursuit of frontier justice to others. Sometimes he permitted himself to dream of going home to South Carolina, of starting all over. Ravenoak, the Torn plantation, was no more, but he could make a place for them, and it would be as though the war that had separated them and all the lonely intervening years had never happened. He could put it all behind him and get on with his life, the way it should have been.

Day before yesterday, in the Southern Saloon, he'd admitted to Carter Bartlett that the law was all he had. But when he found Melony, that would no longer be the case. He would give it up in a heartbeat. Nothing would take him away from her side again. The law was just his mistress. And sometimes, as in this business with the Bartletts, she was hard to please, requiring him to make tough decisions.

The buckskin's soft whicker brought him back to the present.

The horse had stopped grazing and was standing

stock-still now, peering deeper into the trees, ears pricked forward. Something out there. Torn searched the shadows, lifting his hand to shade his eyes from the bright yellow blaze of the campfire.

Three horsemen emerged from the gray twilight, riding slowly, spread well apart, like a skirmish line, holding their horses to a walk.

Slipping the Winchester 44/40 out of its saddle boot, Torn stood up and stepped sideways out of the firelight. They were cowboys, no doubt Slash-B range riders. As they drew closer he saw that neither Clete Bartlett nor Shank Hollis was among them. He didn't recognize any of the three. Had Carter Bartlett really given his boys orders to shoot on sight? Or had that just been a bluff?

I have no quarrel with these men, thought Torn. I don't want to have to kill them. . . .

Then one of the riders drew his side gun, gave a wild and lusty yell, and gadded his horse into a gallop straight for Torn, firing. The other two *brasaderos* followed his lead.

Torn dived for cover behind cypress knees, pursued by hot lead.

CHAPTER 21

DIVING FOR COVER WAS PURE REFLEX. BUT AS HE LAY THERE ON the rocky ground, hearing the bullets thumping into the gnarled roots of the cypress, Torn realized he couldn't hope to make a stand here. The three cowboys were fanning out—they would close in on him from different directions, and he would have no place to hide.

He thought about trying to reach the buckskin, but the horse was hobbled, and he didn't think the Slash-B riders would give him time to remove the hobbles. No, he had to make a run for it. If he could reach the brush, he would find plenty of cover, and the *brasada* would slow his pursuers down. In the darkness he could switch roles with them—could perhaps become the hunter instead of the hunted.

Steeling himself, he jumped up and started running, heading across the creek, away from the three cowboys. He carried the Winchester in his left hand, drawing the Colt Peacemaker and throwing a few shots over his shoulder, just to give them something to think about. They answered with a flurry of rifle fire. Hot lead whined off the rocks covering the creek bed. The rocks made running difficult; several times he stumbled and nearly fell.

He had a few things going for him. The murky twilight impaired the accuracy of their shooting. So did the horses his would-be killers were riding. They were cowponies, trained to work longhorns—they weren't trained to stand steady in the midst of gunfire. Firearms going off close to their heads agitated them. They balked or jumped with every shot, throwing off the aim of the cowboys. And they weren't too surefooted on the rocks. Their iron-shod hooves slipped and clattered on the loose stones. Torn made better time crossing the creek than the horsemen who were after him.

Reaching the chaparral, Torn crouched and emptied the Colt at the cowboys, who were now exposed in the clearing of the creek. Horses and riders were dark shapes against the pale limestone. They couldn't see him in the brush. But they did see the Colt's muzzle flash. Their own weapons spewed yellow flame in the gray gloom.

Torn did not linger long. Bullets clipped the brush around him. Once the Peacemaker was empty, he holstered it and moved on, not spending the time to reload. Crashing deeper into the *brasada,* he almost ran headlong into a stand of cholla. The inch-long spines snagged his frock coat. He fought to pull free, cursing, but couldn't shake loose, and finally shrugged out of the coat.

He ran a minute more, then dropped to one knee and

listened for the sound of pursuit. At first all he could hear was the pounding of his own heart, the rasp of breath in his throat.

One of the cowboys called out from somewhere off to the left, his voice edgy and high-pitched with pain.

"Dell, I'm hit. The sonuvabitch winged me."

"Where did he go?" This came from Torn's right.

"Shut up and keep your eyes open," growled the third rider, also to Torn's right.

A horse whickered. Hooves clacked on stone. Brush rustled, and twigs snapped. Torn started running again.

"There he is!"

The cowboy was closer than Torn had expected him to be. He saw shadows move through an intervening clump of stunted live oak. Muzzle flash accompanied the bark of a rifle. Torn veered off. The ground abruptly dropped away. He fell into a shallow ravine, landing painfully among rocks and cactus. He got up and kept going, limping now, following the ravine.

A horseman broke out of the scrub right on top of him, a black shape against the star-studded indigo sky. Torn fired at point-blank range. The rider cried out and pitched sideways out of the saddle. The horse snorted, shying away. Torn tried to scramble up the bank of the ravine, hoping to catch the cowpony, but he lost his footing and fell. The horse disappeared into the brush.

A gun blazed a few yards to Torn's right, and a bullet whined off rock. Torn cursed himself for a fool. His white shirt was like a beacon in the darkness. Pulling off the saber knife's shoulder rig as he stumbled along the ravine away from the gunfire, he tore the shirt off his back. Pausing to shed the tattered remnants, he picked up his weapons and hurled himself into the *brasada* again.

The brush flayed at his flesh, cutting him dozens of times, but he pressed on, and reached a shelf of sun-blistered limestone that dropped sharply into an arroyo. Again he crouched and listened. At least one of the Slash-B cowboys was still hot on his heels. He could hear the horse crashing through the scrub, a man's soft but fervent curse.

Torn had no choice but to go over the edge. He slipped and slid as loose rock gave way, scraping flesh off hands and elbows as he tried to slow his descent and hold on to the Winchester and saber knife at the same time. Catching his heel in a fissure, he pitched forward, landing clumsily on a narrow ledge thirty feet above the rocky bottom of the arroyo.

Exhausted and in a world of hurt, he dragged himself along the ledge to a place where the shelf jutted out over the arroyo, forming a shallow cave. Above him, the hooves of a horse clattered on the shelf. One of his pursuers was directly overhead.

Trying to quiet his labored breathing, Torn lay still beneath the ledge, waiting. He heard the creak of saddle leather, the thump of bootheels on the shelf. A small avalanche of loose rock debris skittered into the arroyo. The cowboy was standing on the edge, looking over. He couldn't see Torn, who heard another horse approaching.

"Is he down there?"

"If so, I don't see him."

"Dell's dead."

"Christ!"

"The bastard ventilated him."

For a moment neither cowboy spoke. They stood not ten feet above Torn, searching the bottom of the arroyo for sign of their prey.

"We lost him, Tom." Torn heard resignation in the man's voice.

"Yeah. We better get back and tell the old man."

"How bad are you hit?"

"Well, I got a chunk of lead in my arm. It hurts like double-rectified hell. I hate to see the sonuvabitch get away. I'd like to repay the favor."

"He won't get far. We'll take his horse. I reckon tomorrow Mr. Bartlett will have every man who rides for the brand out lookin' for the pilgrim. We'll round him up."

They climbed back into their saddles and rode away.

Torn rolled over on his back, laid his head down, and closed his eyes, letting the tension run out of his punished body.

When he opened his eyes again, it was daylight.

He was so stiff he could hardly move. His upper body was bruised and cut, covered with dried blood. He flexed some of the stiffness out and managed to climb up to the shelf. Returning to the creek, he paused to drink and wash his wounds with cool spring water. He removed a dozen thorns and splinters out of his hide. There were a dozen more that were in too deep and needed to be cut out. He checked the height of the sun and realized it was already midmorning. Aware that by now every range rider on the Slash-B payroll was probably out hunting him, he didn't think it wise to linger in this vicinity. The creek would be the first place they would look, in hopes at least of cutting his trail. The thorns and splinters that remained under his skin were painful, and apt to become infected, but the cutting would have to wait.

Retracing the route he had taken last night to escape the Slash-B cowboys, he found his black frock coat, hanging on the cholla. He worked the garment free, checked for the daguerreotype of Melony Hancock, and breathed a deep sigh of relief when he found it safe and snug in the inside pocket. The photograph meant a lot to him. Aside from a few letters Melony had written him during the war, it was all he had left to remember her by. Sometimes the photograph was the only thing that kept him going in those moments of dark depression when he despaired of ever finding his lost love.

The merciless sun beat down on his back and shoulders, so he donned the torn and tattered coat, strapping the saber knife's shoulder harness on over it. He had lost his hat, too, but found no trace of it.

He sat on his heels in a strip of blackjack shade and pondered the situation. It didn't look good. The Slash-B cowboys had absconded with the buckskin. They'd made off with his saddle, too, leaving him without provisions or extra ammunition.

Rockbottom was two days' ride to the east, and he calculated it would take at least three days to walk that distance. He doubted his ability to elude Carter Bartlett's boys for three days.

Reloading the Colt, he counted his rounds. Eleven more "beans" for the Peacemaker in his gunbelt loops. Add that to the six in the cylinder. The Winchester carried thirteen rounds, and he had no extra 44/40 cartridges.

What did he have? Experience. He'd been through

this kind of thing before. Ten years ago, after breaking out of Point Lookout Prison, he'd been hunted by federal patrols, hounded across Maryland and war-ravaged Virginia. That had been in the closing days of the conflict. Richmond had fallen. Grant's bluecoats were closing in on Lee's ragtag Army of Northern Virginia, at a place called Appomattox Court House. Sherman's men had been swarming all over the Carolinas, crushing pockets of rebel resistance and engaging in wholesale looting and destruction. Through hundreds of miles of devastated, enemy-occupied country, Torn had made his way home. He still didn't quite know how he had managed that, but he had, and now he told himself he could do it again.

A grim determination to succeed and the ability to think clearly and calmly in times of stress were his greatest assets. His years as a cavalry commander had taught him valuable lessons. The Confederate Army had held its own against superior odds for four years. Torn had been witness to military miracles wrought by the likes of Lee, Stuart, and Jackson. They had won by taking risks and boldly doing the unexpected. He decided his best chance for survival in his war with the Slash B lay in following their example.

So when he left the creek, he didn't head for Rockbottom. Instead, he picked up the trail of the cowboys who had ambushed him the night before. He had no trouble following the sign of four horses through the *brasada*. The trail would lead him eventually to the ranch headquarters.

Torn figured that was the last place they would expect him to go.

CHAPTER 22

THE TWO COWBOYS WHO HAD SURVIVED THE DEADLY GAME OF hide-and-seek with Torn traveled well into the night, hoping to ride straight through until they reached the ranch headquarters fifty miles to the northwest. But fifty miles proved to be more than the wounded Tom could manage without a rest. He went as far as he could. Where he fell was the place they made camp.

The range rider who had been the only one lucky enough to emerge from the fight unscathed, a man named Cole, took one look at his *compadre* and knew without a shadow of a doubt that Torn's bullet had to come out of Tom's arm without delay. So he built a fire, heated the blade of a clasp knife, and went to work digging out the slug. That done, he heated the blade again and closed up the wound by laying the white-hot steel against the bullet hole. Finally he dressed the wound with strips of cloth torn from an extra shirt he carried in his saddlebags.

After morning coffee, Tom felt well enough to ride. A little before noon they reached the Slash-B headquarters. The lookouts on the roof of the big house spotted them a quarter mile away. Two riders came out to identify them and one escorted them in while the other rode back with advance word to Carter Bartlett.

The cattle baron was waiting for them out in front of the big house. So were a dozen other hands whose tasks had kept them close to home that day. This included Shank Hollis and the other cowboys who had broken Clete out of the Ellsworth jail.

Carter walked out to the horse bearing the corpse of the man named Dell. The body was lashed down over the saddle and stiff with rigor mortis. His face twisted with grief, Carter put a hand gently on the dead man's back. His sorrow did not escape the notice of the other Slash-B men. No one was surprised. Everyone knew Carter Bartlett cared about his cowboys. That was one reason they gave him their loyalty without reservation. They stood around, tight-lipped, hats in work-callused hands.

Bartlett looked bleakly at Cole. "Torn?"

Cole nodded, downcast. "He got away, Mr. Bartlett. Sorry."

"I know you did the best you could." Carter's pale, piercing eyes flicked to Tom, who was still in his saddle, too weak to dismount, sitting hunched over like a man about to lose his dinner. "Couple of you boys help Tom. Take him into the house."

Two men came forward, pulled Tom as gently as possible out of his hull, and carried him across the sun-whacked hardpan, the wide gallery, and into the house.

"What happened?" Bartlett asked Cole.

"We come up on him yesterday, around sunset. He was camped near Coyote Creek. Bold as brass. Had a big fire going. You could see it two miles off. It was like he didn't give a hoot if anybody knew he was there."

"He didn't," muttered Carter. "The man's got a double dose of grit, I'll give him that."

"You told us to shoot if we found him on Slash-B range," continued Cole, "so we rode in, making smoke. He got off into the chaparral and we went in after him, but we lost him. We brought his horse and gear, though, so he's out there on foot now."

Carter turned his attention to the buckskin, saw the Slash-B brand.

"That looks like the pony Baylis kept out of his string," remarked Slim Taylor from the grim circle of range riders.

"This damned judge must be plumb loco."

The assessment came from Clete Bartlett, who had sauntered out of the big house. "I see ol' Dell crossed the river. You're not going to let Torn get away with that, are you, Pa? You're going to settle his hash, aren't you?"

Cold fury rippled through Carter, setting every nerve ending on fire. Clete didn't seem to be at all upset about Dell's death. He might have been remarking on the weather, for all the concern he showed.

"Why don't you go out and find him and settle his hash, boy?" rasped Carter. "Why don't you do it, man to man?"

Clete's crooked smile was pulled tight as he looked away from his father's angry glare. He scanned the dark and solemn faces of the Slash-B *brasaderos*.

"Well, it ain't just me he's after," he whined, defensive in tone and posture.

"That's a natural fact," agreed Slim. "Mr. Bartlett, I purely hate to do it, but I got an itch to make tracks. Reckon I'll light out for Mexico. I thought we'd all be safe here on the Slash B. Didn't figure anybody would have the gumption to come in here after us, especially after a warning from you. But it ain't so. You warned Judge Torn off and he's coming on, anyroad."

"We can stop him!" railed Wes Holt. "He doesn't stand a chance against us all. I never thought you'd take up henhouse ways, Slim."

Slim scowled. He didn't like being called yellow, particularly by Wes Holt. Holt was a big talker—when he had plenty of help to back him up.

"I'll tag along with you, Slim, if it's okay," said Billy Sheen, with an apologetic glance at Carter Bartlett.

"It's okay, boys," said Carter. "I understand. I'm the one who ought to be saying he's sorry. I am, too. Sorry as hell. I got you all into this."

"Shoot," mumbled Slim, kicking at the dirt. "You done what you thought you had to do, Mr. Bartlett. We've got to do the same, is all."

"If anyone else wants to pull his freight, I won't stand in his way," Carter informed the others. "You can draw your pay and dust out, no hard feelings. You signed on to be cowboys, not gunslingers."

No one spoke up. Finally, a crestfallen Slim Taylor turned and headed for the bunkhouse. Billy Sheen fell in behind him, head hung. Shank Hollis stepped out of the crowd to stand toe to toe with Carter.

"Not you, Shank," whispered Bartlett.

"No, sir. None of this feels right, but you know I'll stick."

Carter nodded, relieved. "I'm going to ride out after Torn in an hour. All those who ride with me, fill your canteens, saddle your best horse, and load your guns."

The cowboys exchanged sober glances, then scattered, some heading for the bunkhouse to get their saddles and rifles, others making for the corrals to cut out their ponies. Shank moved, too, but Carter stopped him.

"You're not going, Shank."

"I'll ride with you, Mr. Bartlett."

"And I'd be proud to have you, but I want you to stay here. With Clete."

"What?" Shank looked across at Clete. It was obvious Carter's son wasn't going to volunteer to join the search for Torn. The idea of staying behind and wet-nursing Clete was almost more than Shank Hollis could bear.

"I'd take it as a personal favor," said Carter, reading the expression on his foreman's face.

"But Torn's probably headed back for Rockbottom," argued Shank. "You don't think he'd try to make it here, do you?"

"Yes, I do. I think that's just what he'll try."

"But that would be crazy."

"Crazy like a fox," replied Carter. "Don't underestimate this man. He'll trail Cole and Tom straight here. I'm going to try to stop him. But he might get through. I'd feel better if you were here."

Shank looked like he had bitten into something sour. But he knew he had no choice. He had always done what Carter had asked of him. It was a habit he couldn't seem to break.

"If that's what you want," he muttered.

Carter put a hand on his shoulder. He appeared unable to find the words to express his gratitude. Clete turned on his heel and disappeared into the house.

An hour later, Shank was standing in the blue shade of the front gallery, smoking a roll-your-own, when Carter and ten Slash-B cowboys rode out. The foreman watched them disappear into the *brasada,* and he kept watching until even their dust had drifted away. Flicking the spent quirly away, he sighed and walked out onto the hardpan to squint up at the roofline. He could see the two lookouts outlined against the brassy sky. One of them waved, and Shank returned the gesture before going into the house.

Clete was over at the long sideboard, pouring himself a drink. "How about a whiskey, Shank?"

"No." Hollis was in no mood to have anything to do with Clete Bartlett. "I think I'll look in on Tom."

"You think Torn will show up here?"

Shank was in the process of leaving the room; now he turned back, curious. He had detected a shrill and shaky note of fear in Clete's voice.

"Maybe," he said.

Clete knocked his drink back, set the empty glass very gently on the sideboard.

"What are you scared of?" asked Shank. "You can handle him if he comes. You don't need a wet nurse. I remember you told me as much, up there in that Kansas hoosegow."

"I ain't scared," hissed Clete. "Don't put your spurs in me, Shank."

Shank's smile was cold and thin, and it aggravated Clete.

"I'm going into town," declared Clete.

"The hell you are."

"The hell I ain't," cried Clete, petulant. "I'm going into town and I'm going to get Caitlin, and we're going to ride for the border."

"You're not going anywhere."

Clete laughed. "That really chaps your hide, doesn't it, Shank? Me running off with Caitlin."

Hollis fought to control himself. "For one thing, she wouldn't go with you."

"Yes, she will. You'll see. I ain't going to hang around here."

"Good men are going out to fight and maybe die for you," said Shank through clenched teeth.

"They'll fight and die for my father, not me. I don't need them or this damn ranch. Or my father, either. I'm leaving."

"No." Hollis laid his hand on the gun at his side. Clete had taken two strides for the door. Shank's hostile move stopped him, but only for a moment.

"You going to kill me, Shank?" Clete leered and shook his head. "I don't think so. You've hated my guts all along. If you'd had your way, I'd be dead and buried in Kansas dirt right now. But you can't kill me. You'd like to so bad it eats away at your insides. But you can't, because it would be just like killing my father. Well, you and he can take this damn ranch and go straight to hell. I'm going to take Caitlin and go to Mexico."

He walked out, and Shank didn't stop him. The Slash-B foreman stood there, stunned. He thought about Caitlin and Clete, together. He wasn't sure about her; maybe she *would* run off with Clete. Loyalty to Carter Bartlett pulled him one way, his love for Caitlin pulled him the other.

And as he stood there, pulled between loyalty and love, something inside Shank Hollis broke.

CHAPTER 23

AFTER WALKING HALF A DAY ACROSS THE TEXAS *BRASADA* IN the middle of summer, Torn was beginning to wonder if he had died and gone to hell.

By midmorning he began to think more about finding water than reaching the Slash-B ranch headquarters. He hadn't come across a spring or creek or a muddy hole in the ground all day and his throat was parched. He cut a pad off a clump of prickly pear and used the saber knife to peel the spines and rubbery green skin away, drawing a little moisture by chewing the fibrous flesh. Finding a little shade beneath a windtwisted cedar, he sat down on a rock to take a rest.

He didn't see the diamondback.

When he heard the rattle, his blood seemed to freeze in his veins. The snake was directly behind him, but he did not dare turn his head to look. The slightest movement on his part might cause the snake to strike.

He sat there, motionless, blinking cold sweat out of

his eyes. His pulse raced, and he couldn't seem to drag enough air into his lungs. He wasn't sure what to do. If he sat perfectly still long enough, would the diamondback lose interest in him? Did he have the nerve to play a waiting game? If he did, would the snake cooperate? And if he tried to jump away, could he move faster than the rattler could strike?

He was sitting with his elbows on knees, hands dangling, and he tried to move his right forearm without any telltale motion in the upper arm or shoulder. His fingers brushed the hilt of the saber knife, sheathed under his left arm. The Colt at his side was out of the question—he would have to pull his arm back for the draw. He moved his right arm another fraction of an inch. Now he could slip the thong off the hilt. The saber knife slipped out of the sheath. The rattling became louder. Or maybe it was just his imagination. A muscle twitched in his shoulder. Another spasmed in his leg. Sweat was rolling down his forehead, stinging his eyes.

Anger welled up inside him. Damned if it didn't seem like the land and everything in it was on Carter Bartlett's side. If that was the way it was going to be, fine. Nothing was going to stop him. Nothing.

He moved, diving forward, twisting at the same time, lashing out behind him with a vicious, desperate lateral stroke of the saber knife. He caught a brief glimpse of the diamondback striking, felt the blade bite. He rolled away, came up in a crouch on trembling legs, a guttural cry wrenched out of his throat, his skin crawling.

He'd cut the rattler in two, six inches behind the wedge-shaped head. Four feet of headless diamondback was writhing on the blood-splattered ground.

Torn sat on his heels and watched until it was still, letting the tension drain out of his body.

"You're one lucky son of a bitch," he muttered to himself.

He cut off the six-inch rattle and put it in his pocket. He had heard it said rattles were good luck.

A few hours later he found out.

He almost walked smack into Carter Bartlett and the Slash-B hands.

Reaching the top of a rise, he saw them on the other side, not a hundred yards away. They were spread out, advancing toward him through the chaparral. There wasn't much brush on the rim of the hill, and for an instant he was caught out in the open. The Slash-B men had sharp eyes. A shout, a rifle shot. Torn turned and ran, heading back down the slope he had just climbed. A loose stone turned under his foot. He lost his balance and fell, crashing through scrub oak, rolling painfully over prickly pear. The Winchester was jarred out of his grasp.

He sprawled to a stop on a cutbank, beyond which lay a sandy dry wash curling around the base of the hill. He got up, dazed and bleeding. Something had laid a deep gash across his right cheek just below the eye. Blood was streaming down his face. More cuts, bruises, and thorns, but nothing broken. He fired a quick glance at the crest of the hill. They were coming hard up the other side—he could hear them. In a minute they would reach the rim. He scanned the slope down which he had just rolled, looking for the rifle, and didn't see it. There wasn't time to search for it.

Hide, run, or fight—those were his choices. How

many riders? He hadn't had time to count, but he figured at least ten. Enough to finish him off. For a moment he seriously considered making a stand. He was tired and hurt and mad as hell. But making a stand was tantamount to giving up. Because if he fought, he would surely die. He hadn't come this far to quit. He had to keep trying.

As he jumped off the cutbank his knee buckled and he rolled in deep sand at the bottom of the wash. Getting up, he saw the shallow hole in the cutbank. Blackjack grew on the edge of the bank, and exposed roots partially screened the cavity.

Torn looked down at himself. His clothes, damp with sweat, were now caked with sand and dun-colored dirt. No, it was a crazy idea. It couldn't possibly work—could it? But how far could he run before they rode him down? And how many could he kill before they killed him? If he stood no chance in flight, and no chance in a fight, then he had to hide. He had to outfox them.

That was it. He was the fox, they were the hounds. And like a fox, he would go to ground.

He was almost certain that Clete Bartlett would be found at the ranch headquarters. Even if Clete were inclined to fight, Carter wouldn't permit it. Torn figured if he could just slip through these cowboys and backtrack them, he might be able to get to Clete and finish the job.

Shrugging out of the saber knife's harness, he shed his tattered coat and used the garment to obliterate his footprints as he walked backward to the hole in the cutbank. He had to worm his way through the tough, resilient blackjack roots. The cavity was large enough that he could stand hunched over. As his head and

shoulders brushed against the top and sides of the
hole, some of the sand and small rocks came down on
top of him. He thrust the saber knife into the roof of the
hole, bringing down even more, until he was buried up
to the knees. Settling back, he transferred the saber
knife to his left hand and drew the Colt with his right.

He could hear them as they came down the hill,
could feel the vibration of their horses' iron-shod
hooves through the ground. More sand sifted down on
top of him, and it occurred to him that the cutbank
might collapse, burying him alive. The clump of blackjack directly above him was small comfort—they
couldn't ride right over him. The weight of horse and
rider might be more than the cutbank could hold.

"Spread out," growled Carter Bartlett. "He can't be
far."

"His trail stops here." This puzzled voice was one
Torn did not recognize.

"Well, he didn't sprout wings and fly," snapped
Carter. "Find him."

Some of the riders followed the dry wash in one direction while others headed the opposite way. They
stayed on the cutbank, and Torn knew they would be
studying the sandy bottom of the wash, looking for his
sign. He could tell that a couple of the *brasaderos* were
lingering overhead. The cutbank was very steep here, a
six-foot drop. He was betting on the fact that getting a
horse down into the wash, at least along this stretch,
would be risky business. Many a horse had broken a
leg, and a many a cowboy his neck, as a result of such
reckless riding.

But one of the Slash-B cowboys had dismounted, and
came so close to the rim of the cutbank that the crust

gave way under his weight. He grabbed hold of the blackjack to keep from falling.

"Be careful, Jess." His *compadre* laughed. "You know you can't swim a lick."

"Very funny," grumbled Jess. "Hey, there's a cave or something down here."

Torn stopped breathing.

"Check it out."

The cowboy wrestled with the blackjack, trying to work his way closer to the hole.

Torn dropped the saber knife, dug into the pocket of his coat, and found the diamondback rattler.

The Slash-B man swore vehemently when he heard the rattle. It was a sound all men on the frontier knew and feared.

"Snake pit," he yelped.

"Get the hell away from there, Jess!"

"You don't have to tell me twice."

Torn felt like laughing out of sheer relief.

But he wasn't out of the woods yet. The Slash-B men combed the area for over an hour. They searched the hill. They crossed the dry wash fifty yards west of the hole in which Torn was hiding. At one point two riders appeared on the bank directly across from the hole, heading east.

Then another hour passed without Torn seeing or hearing any more of them. Had they moved on? He was eager to be out of the hole, but forced himself to be patient. He waited. When he didn't think he could wait any longer, he waited a little more. Nothing. He sheathed the saber knife but kept the Colt ready as he grappled his way through the stubborn blackjack roots.

Climbing out of the dry wash, he ascended the hill. At the top he scanned the *brasada* in every direction.

The Slash-B men had moved on.

Now he took the time to go back down the hill and look for the Winchester. He still couldn't find it, and concluded that one of Carter's men had.

He told himself it didn't matter and bent his steps north by west. Hot, thirsty, bruised, and bloody, he trudged doggedly on, backtracking the cowboys, his goal the ranch headquarters, where he knew he would find Clete Bartlett.

CHAPTER 24

HE NEVER MADE IT TO THE SLASH-B HEADQUARTERS.

Along about sunset he spotted a campfire up ahead, a flicker of flame through the scrub. Moving cautiously closer, he saw two horses, both hobbled, grazing on the sparse grass. A man was sitting back against his overturned saddle, smoking a cigarette and gazing into the crackling fire.

Torn wondered where the second rider was. Two horses usually meant two men. He thought he recognized one of the horses as the buckskin that had carried him down from Kansas, the pony that had once belonged to the cowboy named Baylis.

The man near the fire was facing the other way, and Torn couldn't identify him. Drawing the Colt Peacemaker, he circled the camp, keeping an eye peeled for the second man. In the end-of-day shadows he took a careless step. A brittle twig snapped underfoot. The horses lifted their heads, ears pivoting, and one whickered softly. The man near the fire looked around, but he gave no indication that he was alarmed. When he turned his head, Torn recognized him in the firelight.

Shank Hollis.

"That you, Torn?"

Torn crouched in the brush, his eyes narrow with suspicion. He searched the *brasada,* anticipating ambush.

"Whoever it is," called Hollis calmly, "come on out where I can see you. You're making me nervous. I'm beginning to feel like a long-tailed cat in a room full of rocking chairs."

Still, Torn did not move.

Hollis flicked the cigarette away and slowly stood, holding his arms away from his sides.

"I'm alone, if that's what's got you spooked."

Though he didn't trust Hollis, Torn took a chance. He stepped into the open, into the throw of firelight, the Colt leveled at Shank.

"Unbuckle the gunbelt," he said. "Use your left hand, and move slowly."

Hollis complied.

"Figured it was you, Judge. Had it been a Slash-B hand, he wouldn't have been sneakin' around like a coyote. 'Course, it occurred to me you could be one of them bunch of no-accounts from over in the Concho Breaks. But rustlers usually don't have the backbone for bushwhacking."

The gunbelt dropped, and Hollis obligingly stepped away.

"Where's your partner, Hollis?"

Hollis shook his head. "I'm on my own stick. I brought the buckskin in case I run across you."

"Planned to take me back to Bartlett across the saddle?"

The foreman's expression was positively bleak.

"Don't reckon I ride for Carter Bartlett anymore."

Torn did not reply. He considered the implications of that remark. Intuitively, he felt that Shank was on the level. But it didn't make a whole lot of sense.

"Looks like you've been through hell the long way," observed Hollis. "Carter said you might be able to get through. Guess he read you right. That's why he left me at the house, to keep an eye on Clete. I guess he was counting on me to protect his son from you."

"You rode away?"

"Clete did."

"Where did he go?"

"Rockbottom. Said he was going to get Caitlin, take her to Mexico with him. He knew you were out in the brush, so he saw his chance."

"Caitlin? Caitlin Price?"

Hollis nodded grimly. "You see, Clete thinks Caitlin is sweet on him. I don't know. Maybe she is."

The pure anguish in Shank's voice was telltale.

"You're in love with her," said Torn. It wasn't posed as a question.

The Slash-B foreman's eyes were bright, intense. "I guess so."

Torn made up his mind. He holstered the Peacemaker and moved closer to the fire. "Got any water to spare?"

"Two canteens. Over by my saddle."

Torn drank in moderation. He could have emptied both canteens, as parched as he was, but he exercised self-discipline. The water was warm and brackish, but he couldn't remember ever having tasted sweeter. Hollis remained standing, on the other side of the fire. Torn capped the canteen and picked up Shank's gunbelt.

"So where were you going?"

"Rockbottom," replied Hollis. "I thought I'd try to talk Caitlin out of going with Clete. He doesn't love her. He'll take her across the border and then get tired of her. And then where will she be? Lot of desperate characters down there, Judge. Men who just take what they want. A lot of bad things could happen to her. I don't want that for her."

"There's more to it than that," said Torn, motioning at the buckskin. "You brought that extra horse along for me, or so you say. And you built that fire to draw me in, figuring that if I managed to slip past Bartlett and his crew, I'd backtrack them to the ranch. I've got a hunch you're thinking about keeping Clete and Caitlin apart any way you have to. Even if it means turning Clete over to me. Or maybe even shooting him. How far off the mark am I on this, Hollis?"

Hollis sat on his heels, gazed morosely into the fire.

"Not far. Never thought it would happen. Me turning against Carter Bartlett. You're all the way right, Judge. I would have given Clete to you. 'Course, I expect to go back, too. Back to Kansas, I mean. 'Cause what we did was wrong. I knew it then. But I went ahead."

"Where are the others?"

"Dusted out. On the run for the border. I hope you'll let them go. They're good men, except maybe for Wes Holt. They were just following orders."

"That's no excuse."

"No, I guess not. But you already cost them. They

had to leave the Slash B. They're on the dodge now. That does something to a man. Eats away at his insides."

"And Wes Holt?"

"He's riding with Carter. But the others . . ." Hollis shook his head, sensing that continuing to plead with Torn was a waste of breath.

"Okay," said Torn.

Hollis looked up, surprised. "You mean you'll let 'em go?"

"Did one of them kill Drew Mitchell?"

"That was Wes Holt. And Clete . . . well, Clete put a bullet in him, but he was already dying."

"Then Wes Holt has two choices. Either they bury him here or he hangs in Kansas."

"Reckon I'll hang, too," murmured Hollis. "Maybe I deserve to. As long as I get to see Clete on the gallows next to me—as long as I know he doesn't have Caitlin —I'll be satisfied. Guess that sounds mighty peculiar, doesn't it?"

"Not really," said Torn. He still wasn't clear on the way he felt about Shank Hollis. There could be no denying the fact that Hollis was an accessory in the killing of Drew Mitchell. But Torn felt sorry for the Slash-B foreman. The man had made a big mistake in the name of loyalty—loyalty to Carter Bartlett. That made him different from Clete. Clete had killed because he didn't give a damn about anything or anybody. He was as dangerous as a rabid dog.

"So what now?" asked Hollis.

"You could be lying to me. Clete could still be at the ranch. You could be trying to draw me away."

"You don't trust anybody, do you?"

"Has anybody given me reason to trust him?"

"I won't wrangle that."

Torn tossed the gunbelt to Shank. Then he kicked dirt on the fire, extinguishing the blaze.

"Let's ride," he said.

"To Rockbottom?"

Torn nodded. "If you're talking straight, you'll help me get Clete. If you're not, I reckon you'll try to kill me somewhere between here and town."

"I got the feeling that would be a mistake."

"Yes," said Torn. "Your last."

CHAPTER 25

As she did every day, Caitlin Price took her father's dinner to the Rockbottom jail.

It was her firm belief that Elzy wouldn't eat at all if she didn't remain faithful to this ritual. He ate the meals she cooked only because he felt obliged to; nowadays Elzy's only appetite was for cheap liquor. But Caitlin had resolved never to let him off the hook. In fact, she was convinced that as long as she made him eat, he would stay alive. Without her, he would waste away and die.

It was siesta time in Rockbottom. The town appeared virtually deserted. She spotted one person crossing the street at the other end of town. A couple of horses were tied to hitching posts, suffering in the furnace heat of midday. The sun was a patch of white flame in a sky bleached to a very pale blue.

She didn't see Clete Bartlett. He watched her enter the jail from the deep shade of an alley across the

146

street. His horse was down by Presidio Creek; he wanted to get in and out of town without being noticed. When the door closed behind her, he threw cautious glances both ways before crossing the street with quick, urgent strides, nervously slapping the quirt that dangled from his wrist against a chap-sheathed leg.

Caitlin had put the tray on the desk and was turning toward the cell where, as usual, Elzy Price lay passed out, stone-cold drunk; when Clete barged in, she whirled, gasping, a hand flying to her throat. Clete slammed the door shut behind him and moved to the window to check the street again. Satisfied, he turned and grinned at Caitlin.

"Hello, darlin'. Miss me?"

"Clete!"

"The one and only," he drawled.

"What are you doing here?"

"Why, I came to see my girl." He glanced beyond her, at the unconscious lawman in the cell, and noticed the empty bottle of tequila on the floor beside the bunk. "The old man's still puttin' away the nose paint, I see."

His disrespectful tone of voice made Caitlin bristle. "Don't talk about my father that way."

"Why not? It's the truth, ain't it?"

"Maybe it is. But I don't like it, that's why not."

He crossed the office. "After all these months apart we shouldn't be wasting our time dickering. Give your Clete a kiss."

He grabbed her by the arms and pulled her roughly to him. Caitlin tried to push away, her hands pressing against his chest, but Clete was too strong. He kissed her, none too gently, and she didn't fight. She didn't respond, either. Just submitted. Frowning, Clete finally let her go and backed off.

"What's the matter with you?" he asked testily. "Ain't you glad to see me?"

She wiped her mouth with the back of a hand. "Of course I'm glad to see you, Clete. But I'm not some dance-hall girl, so don't try to take any liberties with me."

"Well, excuse the hell out of me."

"All I'm asking for is a little respect," she explained, relenting.

Clete's gaze roamed boldly over her. Caitlin felt as though he were undressing her with his eyes.

"Oh, I respect every inch of you, lady," he said, leering.

"What are you doing here, Clete?"

"I've come to take you away."

"Away?"

"Yeah. Away from all this. You don't want to waste your whole life in this stinking town, do you? Waiting on that old drunk hand and foot? You oughta have better. So you're coming with me."

"Where?" asked Caitlin, stunned.

"Wherever I want to go. I go where I please. I don't answer to nobody. What does it matter to you, long as you're with me?"

"Is your father sending you away because of that man, that judge?"

"My father don't tell me what to do anymore," snapped Clete.

Caitlin's voice was very soft and intense. "Clete, did you kill that man in Kansas?"

"It was an accident. So some old man is dead. So

what? It's done. I can't change that. Not even by hanging. I don't know why everybody has to get all worked up about it."

Caitlin stared, astounded.

"You don't mean that," she whispered.

"I mean every word." Clete scowled darkly. "Now I'm riding for Mexico, and you're going with me."

"I take it you're telling me," she said coolly. "Not asking."

"Okay. Fine. I'll ask, if that'll make you feel any better." Clete snorted, shaking his head. "Will you come with me to Mexico, Caitlin?" He posed the question without a trace of sincerity in his voice.

She took a deep breath. "No."

Clete couldn't believe his ears. "What?"

"The answer is no."

"Why the hell not?"

"Because I won't leave my father. He needs me. He'll die without someone to take care of him, and I'm all he has."

Clete blushed with anger. He grabbed her again, this time more roughly than before. And this time she fought, slapping him so hard his head snapped back. Shocked and hurting, Clete released her and retreated, throwing a hand up to protect his face in case she pressed the attack.

"Get out," she said.

Injured pride ignited blind rage in Clete. Glaring sullenly at Caitlin, he drew his side gun.

At first, Caitlin thought he was going to shoot her. But Clete brushed past her, into the open cell where Elzy Price still lay sound asleep. Before Caitlin could react, Clete had the gun aimed at Elzy's head and was thumbing the trigger back.

"If this drunken sonuvabitch is all that's keeping you here," snarled Clete, "I'll just kill him."

"No!" screamed Caitlin.

Her cry pierced the whiskey-dulled mind of Elzy Price. The besodden sheriff woke with a start. Both Caitlin's scream and Elzy's sudden, unexpected movement startled Clete. He took a step back from the bunk, his nerves jangled.

Elzy rolled and fell off the bunk. Groggy and bleary-eyed, he looked up at Clete, trying to focus. Clete recovered from his surprise and landed a vicious kick in Elzy's ribs. Price wheezed, moaned, and flopped over on his back, white as a boiled shirt, wrapping his arms around his midsection. Wearing an ugly grin, Clete stepped in to deliver another kick.

Caitlin plowed into him before he could do more damage to Price. She scratched and kicked and screamed at him like a wounded wildcat. Clete was driven against the cell wall by the fury of her attack. When she raked at his eyes with her clawing fingers, he hit her with his fist, cursing her. She went down, but got right back up, wiping blood from a cut lip. Behind a veil of tousled copper-colored hair, her pale blue eyes seemed to turn several shades darker. They shot daggers of icy hate at Clete.

"You bastard," she breathed.

He pointed the gun at Elzy again. Price was still curled up on the floor, grunting.

"Woman, are you coming with me or not?" hissed Clete.

There was no doubt in Caitlin's mind that he would shoot her father.

She realized then how wrong she had been about Clete. Something about him, his wild and carefree ways, had attracted and excited her. Sometimes she had longed to be a little wild and carefree herself, those days when she thought life was passing her by. She was human; she couldn't help feeling a little resentful on occasion, buried in a backwater town looking after a man who acted like he didn't care about anything except where his next bottle was coming from.

Sure, she had heard the talk about Clete—that he had bad blood, that he was crazy mean. But she'd thought it was only talk and had convinced herself that Clete Bartlett was just a misunderstood free spirit. But now she saw him for what he really was. Not an impetuous, headstrong boy, but a vicious, evil creature.

"Don't hurt him," she said. "I'll go with you, Clete. Just don't hurt my father. Please. I beg you."

Clete grinned, sensing that he had the upper hand. He looked with scorn at Elzy Price and felt an almost overpowering urge to pull the trigger. He could kill Price and take Caitlin whether she wanted to go with him or not. He didn't have to bargain with her. Who did she think she was, anyway, making conditions?

Her plea did not restrain him; the fact that a gunshot would bring the whole town running did. He wanted to get out of Rockbottom undetected. Didn't want to leave any kind of trail for that stubborn bastard Torn to latch onto.

So he holstered his six-gun, grabbed Caitlin, and marched her across the office to the front door. His grip hurt her, but Caitlin didn't cry out. She didn't resist. She didn't want to do anything that might set Clete off, afraid that he would kill her father if she did.

She looked back once through silent tears as Clete manhandled her through the door. Somehow she just knew she would never see her father again.

Outside, Clete pulled up short.

Torn and Shank were riding down the street.

CHAPTER 26

When he saw Clete Bartlett emerge from the Rockbottom jail, Torn reacted by drawing the Colt Peacemaker. It was a reflex action and, in retrospect, the wrong move to make. Clete swung Caitlin around in front of him, clenched her to him with an arm around her waist. He held her so tightly that she gasped for breath. As Clete drew his own gun Torn realized his mistake. He didn't dare return fire if Clete started shooting, for fear of hitting Caitlin.

The fact that Clete and Torn both drew iron alarmed Shank Hollis; all he could think about was Caitlin's safety. Nothing else mattered.

"Don't shoot!" he yelled, frantic. "For God's sake, don't shoot!"

He reined his horse sharply around in front of Torn's buckskin, placing himself in the line of fire. Clete fired anyway. As Shank slumped forward in the saddle Caitlin screamed. Torn put the Colt away, leaned out, and grabbed the reins out of Shank's hand. Clete fired a second time, but this shot went wild. Torn managed to lead Shank's horse into an alley.

Dismounting, Torn helped Hollis down. The Slash-B foreman sagged. Clete's bullet had struck him in the shoulder at an upward slant. Blood was beginning to stain the back of his shirt, and by this Torn knew that the slug had passed clean through. It was not, in all likelihood, a mortal wound if it was tended to quickly, but any man struck by a .45-caliber bullet was going to have the starch taken out of him. Torn tried to let Shank down to the ground as gently as possible. As he started to move away Hollis found enough strength to grab his arm and detain him.

"Caitlin," gasped Shank. "Don't . . ."

"I won't," said Torn, pulling free.

He realized he was making promises again, promises he wasn't sure he could keep. Hollis wanted his assurance that nothing would happen to Caitlin Price. Torn could recall a very similar situation, weeks ago in Ellsworth, when he had assured Jenny that nothing would befall Drew Mitchell. He had failed miserably on that occasion; would he fare any better this time around?

Moving to the end of the alley, he chanced a look around the corner. A bullet smacked into the adobe inches from his head. Clete was trying to get across the street, but he wasn't making very good time, because he was walking backward while holding Caitlin in front of him, a human shield. He had been waiting for Torn to stick his neck out.

Muttering a soft but fervent epithet, Torn pulled back out of Clete's sight, his back to the wall. The thought of Clete escaping stuck in his craw. After all he had been through to track this man down, Torn was unwilling to let him just walk away without a fight. But what could he do? In a shoot-out Caitlin would almost certainly catch a bullet.

His only choice seemed to be to let Clete ride out of Rockbottom. Shank had said Clete was bound for Mexico. Torn told himself he would just have to keep tracking him, even if it took him south of the border, even if it took weeks, months. Forever.

Or he could try to goad Clete into fighting like a man.

He didn't think it would work. Clete didn't have the guts. And there was terrible risk involved.

But Torn was sick and tired of the manhunt, and in the end decided to take the risk.

Leaving the Peacemaker in its holster, he stepped out into the street. Clete was nearly across to the other side. Torn was vaguely aware of people coming cautiously out of doorways up and down the street, but they were keeping their distance, and he kept his attention riveted on Clete. He saw Clete's gun swing around and got ready to throw himself to the ground. But when Clete saw Torn's gun was holstered, he hesitated to pull the trigger.

"Let her go," said Torn. It had the ring of an order, rather than an appeal.

"Stay back!" rasped Clete.

"For once, Bartlett, fight like a man. Only a coward hides behind a woman."

"Go to hell!"

Elzy Price stumbled out of the jail. He was doubled over, both arms wrapped around his chest.

"Daddy, go back!" cried Caitlin.

"Clete," growled Elzy, "let go of my girl."

Clete's charcoal burner swung toward Price. But that didn't stop Elzy. His expression one of grim resolve, he started across the street, straight at Clete.

"I'll kill you!" bawled Clete. "I swear, old man, I'll put a bullet in you, so help me."

Elzy kept coming on. "Get your filthy hands off my daughter."

Caitlin began to struggle, desperately trying to break free from Clete.

"Price, no!" barked Torn.

He could see it coming. He knew what was going to happen: Elzy was walking into certain death. The sheriff's gun was still in its holster, but Torn doubted that this would constrain Clete. Price was pushing hard, too hard, and Clete was teetering on the brink of panic. He was having difficulty holding on to Caitlin. He was losing his grip on the situation as well.

But Price seemed not to hear Torn's warning. He tried to straighten up, wincing with pain.

Torn thought he had never seen a man walk taller.

"Daddy, stop!" begged Caitlin, tears streaming down her cheeks. "He'll kill you. Oh God, please . . ."

Clete could no longer hold her, so he shoved her away. She stumbled and fell. Price clawed for his side gun. He had no chance. Clete fired, dogged the hammer back, and fired again. Elzy dropped to his knees, taking the first bullet in the belly. The second hit him higher, in the chest, and slammed him backward into the dust.

Torn drew the Colt Peacemaker and fired. Clete was already turning to make a dash down the alley. The slug hit him in the small of the back. He pitched forward on his face, got up, and staggered like a drunken man into the alley. Torn broke into a run. Clete made it halfway down the alley before the earth tilted so bad that he had to slump against a wall. He looked up as Torn approached. His gun arm dangled, and he made no attempt to bring his pistol to bear.

"Drop it or use it," said Torn.

"Don't shoot," croaked Clete. "Christ, it hurts! You done me in."

"You're getting my hopes up."

Clete started to slip down the wall. He dug his heels into the ground, trying to hold himself up. He still held the gun.

Part of Torn wanted to kill Clete here and now, whether Clete dropped the gun or not. The man was going to hang anyway. It would save everybody a lot of trouble. But something held him back. It was the law. His mistress. If he didn't do this right, he wouldn't be any better than Clete Bartlett. But would he ever get Clete back to Kansas? What were his chances, against Carter Bartlett and the Slash-B men? What if they kill me? Torn asked himself.

Then Clete gets away with murder.

"You're going to hang, boy," he said. "Ever seen a man hanged? His tongue swells up and sticks out of his mouth. His face turns blue. Blood vessels pop. He dances on the end of the rope, trying to touch the ground. If the drop doesn't break his neck—and, you know, it doesn't always—then he strangles to death, trying to suck air into his lungs. It's a gruesome sight, Clete. But the worst part is the smell. Because when he's dying, a man loses control of his bodily functions. He soils himself. He—"

Screaming, Clete brought the gun up.

The Colt jumped in Torn's hand. In the narrow alley, the gunshot was loud in his ears. He saw the puff of dust off Clete's shirt as the bullet struck home.

Clete sat down, leaving a crimson streak of blood on the adobe wall, then slumped sideways, dead eyes staring into hell.

Torn drew a deep breath, nodded, and walked back out to the street.

Caitlin was kneeling beside Elzy Price. Torn crossed over to stand beside her. Elzy was still alive, but Torn knew in a glance that he wasn't going to stay that way much longer. Price squeezed Caitlin's hand.

"Don't cry, girl," he whispered. "You know, this is the way every Texas Ranger wants to go. With his boots on."

"I was wrong about you, Price," said Torn. "That was a mighty brave thing you did."

Elzy's eyes were filled with gratitude. "I'm just sorry . . . sorry . . . leave my little girl alone . . ."

"She won't be," said Torn. "I know a man, a damned good man, who loves her very much."

Elzy sighed and closed his eyes for good.

CHAPTER 27

THE NEXT DAY TORN DROPPED BY THE DOCTOR'S OFFICE, located in a small two-room stone house at the edge of town, to look in on Shank Hollis.

He walked in on an altercation.

The doctor lived in the back room and conducted his business in the front, which contained a desk, a glass-fronted cabinet containing medicine and books, and a small bed behind a folding screen for those occasions when the doctor had a patient who required constant supervision. It was in this bed that Torn had expected to find Hollis.

But Shank was sitting in a chair half-dressed; he had his trousers and one boot on, and he was having trouble getting the other boot on while at the same time keeping the doctor covered with his six-gun.

"Thank God you're here!" cried the sawbones in vast relief as Torn entered the room.

Dumbstruck, Torn stood there a moment. The doctor was backed up against a wall, his hands raised. On the other side of the room, Shank swore softly as he tried to stomp his foot into the boot. His chest and shoulder were tightly bandaged, the left arm immobilized in a sling, and his one free hand was full of shooting iron.

"Don't just stand there," reproved the doctor. "Do something."

"Hollis." Torn sighed. "What do you think you're doing?"

"He said he was going to tie me down if I tried to get up," said Shank.

"Hollis, you mulehead," snapped the doctor, thoroughly exasperated. "If you open that wound, I swear to heaven above I'm just going to let you bleed to death and be done with you."

"I'm going to Elzy Price's funeral," said Shank, with quiet resolve.

"Put that gun away," said Torn firmly. "As for you, Doc, you might as well give up trying to keep this man down."

"But he needs to stay in bed at least a week. He . . ." The doctor shook his head. "Fine. Go ahead and kill yourself, Shank."

The doctor stormed out. Shank put the gun down, looking sheepish.

"I guess I shouldn't have done that. But damn it, Torn, I've just got to be at that buryin'. I can't lie here and let Caitlin go through that on her own."

"I know. Don't worry about me. I'm not going to try to stop you."

Shank finally got the boot on and stood up slowly. He was none too steady on his feet and winced as he reached for the shirt draped over the back of the chair. Torn helped him put the shirt on.

"You look a long sight better than you did," remarked Hollis.

Torn had bought a new pair of black trousers, a white shirt, now closed at the throat with a black string tie, and a black broadcloth coat to conceal the saber knife in its shoulder harness. The doctor had seen to his injuries yesterday, removing numerous splinters and cactus spines, applying a salve to his various cuts and abrasions, and closing the deep gash on his cheek with three stitches.

"Can't say the same for you," Torn said. Hollis was pale and haggard, and as wobbly as a just-born foal.

"I'll make it." Realizing that buckling on his gunbelt with one hand was an exercise in futility, Hollis shoved the six-gun under the waistband of his pants.

"Expecting the doctor to ambush you on the way out?" asked Torn, smiling.

"I'm expecting Carter Bartlett. You know someone's bound to have ridden out to the Slash B with word of what happened. Why don't you get while the getting's good, Judge? Hasn't there been enough killing?"

Torn's smile melted. "Wes Holt."

Shank grimaced. "Hombre, you know what your problem is? You don't know when to quit."

"It isn't your fight."

"You're dead wrong. When Carter finds out I helped you, it'll be mine, all right. That's an ironclad guarantee."

"What are you going to do?"

"I reckon I'll shoot back when I get shot at. It won't

be easy. I know all the boys who ride with Carter. You got a better idea?"

"I mean after."

"Well, assuming Carter doesn't kill me, I'll be taking a little ride to Kansas. Give those folks up there a chance to curl my toes."

"I don't think so," said Torn.

Hollis stared. "What did you say?"

"You heard me. You're not going to Kansas."

"Look, I didn't kill that sheriff, but I was in charge. I won't try to get out from under that."

"I never heard a man argue *for* a noose around his neck before. Shank, I don't ever want to see you in Kansas. That goes for the others who were in on the jailbreak. If you happen to run across any of them, be sure to tell them that."

"Except Wes Holt."

Torn nodded. "So I'll ask you again. What are you going to do? Where do you think you and Caitlin will go?"

Some color appeared under Shank's cheekbones.

"That's getting mighty personal," he mumbled.

"I know she came to see you yesterday, and again this morning. Don't tell me you don't have the guts to ask her."

"Ask her what?"

"You *are* a mulehead."

"Now, wait a minute—"

"No. Listen good." Torn pointed a finger at Hollis. "I promised Elzy Price, right before he died, that you were going to look after his daughter. If you don't aim to do that, then I'll just haul your butt to Kansas after all."

Hollis looked down at his boots, embarrassed. "Well, I do have a little money saved up. Enough to start a little place of our own. At first, just a couple hundred head. I don't know where, exactly. It'll have to be a long way out of Carter Bartlett's shadow. But hell, I don't even know if she'll—"

"She will," said Torn.

Hollis gave him a blank look.

"You know something, Judge?"

"What's that?"

"I knew you were trouble on wheels the first time I laid eyes on you."

Torn grinned.

Shank grinned right back at him.

One day later, Uvaldo, the Slash-B grubslinger, rolled through Rockbottom in the chuckwagon, on his way to the ranch.

Torn was sitting on a bench in front of the hotel, taking advantage of a little shade that was steadily dwindling as the day advanced. He had been there since shortly after sunrise. The townfolk were avoiding him like the plague. They knew what he was waiting for— what was coming. He just sat there, his long legs stretched out and crossed at the ankles, his hat pulled down over his eyes, and people remarked he had to be crazy or cold-blooded to sit there so nonchalantly when he knew he was about to die.

When the chuckwagon trundled down the street, he got up and walked out to intercept it. Uvaldo climbed the leathers to stop his mules and stared at Torn in total surprise.

"Madre de Dios! You are still alive. It is a miracle."

"Must be."

Uvaldo looked around, noticed how deserted the town looked. It wasn't yet time for the siesta. The only explanation, then, was that the people of Rockbottom were expecting violence. The old Mexican, wise in the ways of the frontier, could feel the tension in the hot, still air.

"*Qué pasa, hombre?*"

"Clete Bartlett is dead."

"You kill him?"

Torn nodded. "The undertaker's got the body. Folks seemed to think Carter Bartlett would want his son's remains buried in Slash-B ground. So we're waiting for him. But Clete's getting pretty ripe. Maybe you ought to take him back with you."

"*Sí.* I will do this thing. What should I tell Señor Bartlett?"

"Tell him what happened. And tell him I want Wes Holt."

"You are loco, hombre. Señor Bartlett will come with all his *brasaderos*. You will stand alone against all those guns?"

Torn's smile was about as warm as a high-country winter.

"If I have to."

"Well, the Texas Rangers, they have a saying: One fight, one man."

Torn thought of Elzy Price, cold in his grave not a hundred yards from where he stood. He wondered if Uvaldo was aware that Price had been the source for that saying.

"So I've heard," he replied.

"I go now," said Uvaldo. "I will bring Señor Bartlett

his son's body. And then I will come back here, hombre, with the others. I told you I would give you a decent burial. A brave man deserves that, at least. *Vaya con Dios.*"

He whipped up the mules and rolled on, leaving Torn to stand alone in the dusty street.

CHAPTER 28

THEY ARRIVED LATE THE FOLLOWING AFTERNOON. TORN WAS IN the Southern Saloon, having a drink, a shot of whiskey. It wasn't Carter Bartlett's bonded bourbon, unfortunately. Torn didn't think it would be proper to drink a man's liquor after having shot and killed his son. Not that the bartender would have obliged him anyway.

A man came running in with the news, the words gushing out in breathless excitement. But when he saw Torn standing at the bar, one booted foot hooked over the brass rail cleated to the bottom of the mahogany, the man became deathly pale. His eyes widened. His mouth opened and closed, opened and closed, but no further sound emerged. He looked like he'd just been punched in the breadbasket and was trying to haul air into his lungs.

Aside from the bartender and Torn, there were two others in the long narrow room, with its green tin ceiling and pier glass and the faro rig in the back. This duo was occupying one of the deal tables. They had done very little talking since Torn's arrival. His presence had put a damper on their conversation, but they were too curious about him to leave. He could see their reflections in the pier glass behind the bar. They had been watching him, their expressions sullen if not hostile. Now they exchanged alarmed glances. Their chairs scraped on the floor as they got up, and they made a quick exit, followed by the speechless bearer of bad tidings.

Torn knocked back the last of his whiskey and glanced at the barkeep. The barkeep put the bottle from which he had poured Torn's drink on the bar. He hadn't been very friendly either, but Torn saw this gesture as a small courtesy. The bartender no doubt believed that every man who was about to meet his Maker deserved one free drink on the house. The barkeep walked to the end of the mahogany, lifted the hinged gate, and disappeared into the back room.

Torn looked at the bottle, considered helping himself to another drink, decided against it. He didn't need any ninety-proof nerve medicine. His nerves were in fine shape. Ever since his first action in the war—his baptism of blood—he had discovered within himself the ability to go into battle calm, cool, and collected.

As he turned toward the door he noticed for the first time, a few feet down the bar from where he stood, that someone had taken a knife and carved a "/B" into the top of the mahogany. He hadn't seen it before, in among all the other scars and stains and graffiti. A wry smile turned the corners of his mouth. Was there anything, or anyone, that Carter Bartlett didn't have his brand on?

Stepping out into the bright heat, he looked upstreet and saw them. Bartlett was in the lead. Ten *brasaderos* followed him. Bringing up the rear was Uvaldo, on one of his mules. They were all holding their mounts to a walk. Most of the range riders had their saddle guns drawn. A pall of yellow dust was suspended in the still air behind them. They themselves were covered head to toe with dust. Their horses looked worn-out. So did they. Torn figured they'd spent all this time out in the *brasada* hunting for him.

He was glad the waiting was over.

A momentary regret cut through him, and he was conscious of the shape and weight of the daguerreotype in the pocket of his coat. Now he would never find Melony. He felt as though he were betraying her by going out to die in this Texas street. It was betrayal because his mistress, Justice, was compelling him to see this through, even though there wasn't a chance of his surviving. He could not resist her. She had asked a lot of him in the past, and now she was asking for the most a man could give.

He walked out into the middle of street.

Carter checked his horse thirty feet away. His gimlet eyes bored straight through Torn, bright and burning with hate. The Slash-B riders fanned out on both sides of him, making a single line that stretched almost from boardwalk to boardwalk.

For a moment no one spoke. Torn took it upon himself to break the tense silence.

"Which one of you is Wes Holt?"

The cowboy immediately to Carter's right reacted to this sharp-spoken query, answering Torn's question.

Holt threw a worried glance at Bartlett, and nervously slapped his chap-covered leg with a quirt of braided rawhide. Torn thought it was the same quirt he had seen Clete carry, the one that had been among the personal effects Uvaldo had taken possession of yesterday, along with Clete's corpse.

"You're under arrest, Holt," said Torn, "for the murder of Sheriff Drew Mitchell."

Holt tried to laugh at that, but he looked and sounded like he was choking, not laughing.

"You killed my son," said Carter, hollow-voiced, staring at Torn.

"I say we hang him!" exclaimed Holt.

"No."

This came from Shank Hollis. Every head turned as Hollis stepped out of an alley and crossed the street to stand beside Torn. He was weak, unsteady, but he made it.

"Get out of here," snapped Torn.

Shank shook his head stubbornly. "I told you. This is my fight, too."

"What about Caitlin? Think about her."

"I am. She deserves a man who stands up for what's right. It's about time I did that. Besides, you don't have much call trying to talk sense to me. I mean, look at you, Judge. Standing here with eleven-to-one odds against you. That doesn't strike me as very sensible. At least now the odds are cut in half."

"Shank," groaned Carter. "I never thought you'd betray me. Not you."

"You were wrong from the very start, Mr. Bartlett. And so was I for going along with it. We're the ones to blame for everything's that happened. Not this man. Can't you see? You can see it by the way he stands here, against all of you. Only a man who has right on his side could stand here like this."

"My son is dead," muttered Carter, tall and unbending in the saddle.

"Been a lot of killing," said Shank. "Too much. More won't change a damn thing. Look at these men, Mr. Bartlett. They'd all ride into hellfire for you. They'll die for you, too. Just say the word. Baylis, Casey, Dell—they all died for you. You did your best for Clete, sir. You gave him every chance and then some. But he just had bad blood in him. Why spill good blood for bad? Clete's dead. It was bound to happen this way, and there was nothing you could do to keep it from happening." Shank glanced at Torn. "Revenge hasn't ever done anybody a bit of good. I say we live and let live."

Carter looked left and then right, at the dark, dusty faces of the Slash-B cowboys. They were troubled by the fact that Shank Hollis was standing against them. His words made sense. But they were still bound to do what Carter Bartlett told them to.

It was, Torn knew, the moment of truth. It was all in Bartlett's hands. A tremendous inner struggle wrenched at the cattleman's craggy features, as reason and conscience battled grief and rage and the instinct to strike back. In spite of the situation, Torn felt sorry for the man.

"Live and let live," murmured Bartlett, nodding. "Maybe you're right, Shank. Maybe it's time for that."

Cursing, Wes Holt jerked on the reins, trying to turn his horse out of line, but the animal collided with Bartlett's mount, creating turmoil. Torn moved quickly, plowing into the confusion, reaching up to grab Holt, intent on dragging him out of the saddle. Holt laid into him with the quirt. The braided rawhide slashed the side of Torn's neck, drawing blood. Torn ignored the searing pain and pulled the cowboy down. Holt's horse jumped sideways as Bartlett's sorrel snapped at it, hit Torn from behind as he drew the Colt Peacemaker. Torn stumbled over Holt and lost his grip on the gun. Holt scrambled to his feet and clawed for his own six-shooter. He was a shade too slow. Torn moved like lightning. The blade of his saber knife flashed in the blazing Texas sun.

He got in close enough, fast enough, to knock Holt's hogleg down as it went off, and was about to drive the saber knife into the range rider, a killing blow, when at the last possible fraction of a second he changed his mind and altered the angle of the knife stroke. The blade bit deeply into Holt's gun arm, striking the bone. Holt let out a squall. The gun slipped from numb, use-less fingers. He stumbled backward, fell, blood spurt-ing from the knife wound and darkly staining the pale dust of the street.

Torn threw a quick look along the line of Slash-B cowboys, his attention drawn by the all-too-familiar sound of rifle actions. At the same time he was aware of Shank Hollis drawing his own gun.

"No shooting!" bellowed Carter. "Put those irons away!"

The *brasaderos* obeyed.

"Take Wes back to Kansas," Bartlett told Torn. "Take him, and get the hell out of Texas."

Torn didn't like to be told to get out of anywhere, but he couldn't blame Carter. After all, he had killed the man's son. He couldn't expect an invitation to supper.

So he nodded, willing to accept the condition, indulging Bartlett.

Carter turned his attention to Shank. His expression softened.

"I'd be obliged if you'd come back to the Slash B," he said gruffly.

"Caitlin Price and I are going to be married," said Shank.

Carter looked surprised. And then he looked pleased.

"Good. That's just fine. You're both welcome. You can be a husband and a foreman at the same time, can't you?"

"I'll think on it," said Hollis, grateful.

"It's your home, Shank."

Carter turned his horse and rode away, followed by the Slash-B cowboys.

Uvaldo lingered in the drift of their dust. He nodded at Torn, and Torn nodded back. The old Mexican wrestled the mule around in the right direction and kicked it into a bone-jarring gait.

Hollis was moving away, too, as fast as he could in his weakened condition. Torn could see why: Caitlin was running to meet him. One of these days, hoped Torn, he would be as lucky as Hollis, and Melony would fly into his arms just the way Caitlin was flying into Shank's.

One of these days.

But for now he had a job to do. He went to Wes Holt. The wounded cowboy was writhing in agony on the ground. Torn took off his string tie, used it as a tourniquet on Holt's injured arm.

The bleeding finally stopped.